A HEART
SET FREE

BY

NICOLA WEST

MILLS & BOON LIMITED
ETON HOUSE   18-24 PARADISE ROAD
RICHMOND   SURREY   TW9 1SR

First published in Great Britain 1992
by Mills & Boon Limited

© Nicola West 1992

Australian copyright 1992
Philippine copyright 1992
This edition 1992

ISBN 0 263 77513 5

Set in Times Roman 10½ on 12 pt.
01-9204-53143 C

Made and printed in Great Britain

CHAPTER ONE

THE lake was calm and quiet as Laurie drove carefully down the last few yards of the track and stopped her car at the edge of the little paper-birch grove. She sat for a moment as the last notes of the engine died away, listening to the silence that was, in fact, no silence at all but simply a different quality of sound. Her city-tuned ears gradually adjusted themselves to the absence of traffic noise, the sonorous hum that sounded even at the dead of night, and she began to hear the sounds of the lake instead. The singing of birds in the trees, the sudden buzz of a humming-bird's wings, and then, like a faint lament across the darkening waters, the cry of the loon.

Laurie caught her breath. Quietly, she got out of the car and walked down to the water's edge. It was stained now with the deep coppery red of the sunset that glowed at the far end of the lake. On the far shore, the rounded contours of the hills were black against the sky, broken by the shaggy silhouettes of trees.

The loon called again. She peered into the burning dusk, knowing that she was unlikely to see the big black bird swimming low in the water. But its cry, wild and lonely like the sound of some ancient woodwind instrument, seemed to welcome her home. It was the sound of the lake itself.

Away to her left, towards the head of the lake, she saw the first few scattered islands, thick with clusters of trees. And, as she gazed, she saw a tiny point of light spark out suddenly from the midst of one of those clusters. It glowed like the darting lights of the fireflies that were beginning to appear, and she stared at it, feeling a strange sensation tingle down her spine.

It was probably a cottage, she thought, a cottage just like her own, used for holidays and weekends. Some of the islands did have them. But she had never seen a light on one of these islands before. There had never been a cottage there when she'd used to come here with her parents and the Brandon family.

Campers? But there was something about the light that told her it wasn't campers. And she had an odd, disturbing feeling that whoever it was out there was watching her.

Laurie turned away. It was the silence, the isolation—after all these years of city life, she wasn't accustomed to it. For a few minutes she stood watching the flickering green lights of the fireflies. Then, turning away from the darkness, she walked back up the twisting little path through the grove of paper-birch trees, went up the steps and entered the cottage her parents had built so many years ago.

Laurie slept very little that first night she spent at the lake. It was as if by coming here she had undammed a flood of memories, memories that went back into the past and were too painful to examine, so that she had to concentrate on more recent ones. And even those were uncomfortable and difficult to face. But she was beginning to realise that until she had faced them—all of them—she would have no peace. And so she sighed, turned over on to her back, and let the thoughts flow.

And, as she had known he must, Russ Brandon dominated those thoughts.

He had come back into her life after seventeen years, just when she least expected—or wanted—him. Driving his way back into her thoughts when she had only just begun to wear Alec's ring, when any man would be unwelcome, and a man such as Russ Brandon, with his air of wild virility, could be a real threat. Not that she'd ever seen him as a threat—not to begin with. And even now...

Laurie turned restlessly in her bed. Why did she think of Russ as being a threat? He hadn't broken up her relationship with Alec—that had been due entirely to her realisation that they were unsuited. And Russ hadn't played any part in that at all—had he?

But if he hadn't come to Aunt Ella's house that evening in Ottawa, just before Canada Day, would Laurie have come to that realisation? Perhaps not. Perhaps she would have gone ahead and married Alec and been his society wife, hostess to his business acquaintances, mother of his children... perhaps she would never have known...

But it *wasn't* Russ who had caused the break, she argued fiercely. It was the cottage—this cottage. And her mind went back to that day at the end of June, when she had brought Alec to Ottawa to introduce him to the uncle and aunt who had brought her up.

'Well, you've done very well for yourself, Laurie,' Ella Marchant said approvingly as Laurie helped her stack the dishwasher after dinner. 'Alec's a fine man. And if he's a managing director at—how old is he?'

'Forty.' Laurie had been slightly uneasy about this. 'You don't think he's too old for me?'

'At forty? Of course not. A woman needs an older man. Especially a woman like you, Laurie. And you'll have none of the early struggles to make ends meet that so many young people have. No, I think the age-gap is just right. And I should know—your uncle John is twelve years older than me.' She put the last plate into the machine and straightened up. 'You need a man you can look up to and respect—all this modern liberation is all very well, but when it comes to a crisis a man will always take charge.'

Laurie looked at her and wondered what some of her friends would say if they could hear those words. They didn't believe anyone really thought like that these days. They believed in equality, in a woman's right to run her own life. They believed that a woman was as capable of coping in a crisis as any man.

Laurie smiled at her aunt and turned to follow her back to the living-room, where Alec was sitting back in a large armchair watching John Marchant pour two brandies. They glanced up and smiled as the two women entered the room, but did not pause in their discussion.

'Myself, I think the Government's quite right,' John was saying. 'Those new measures should effectively quash any opposition. People have got to realise that things can't be allowed to go on in the lax manner they have until now.'

'Absolutely.' Alec sipped his brandy. 'But that's the trouble these days. People *are* so lax. Schools, colleges, even in the workplace, there's simply no discipline. Someone has to take the lead.' He turned and smiled at Laurie. 'But you two don't want to hear dull talk like this. Tell me about this party you've got arranged for tomorrow evening.'

'Oh, it's not going to be anything grand,' Ella said deprecatingly. 'Just a few old friends, people who've known Laurie for years and will like to meet you and celebrate your engagement. And I must say, Alec, that really is a beautiful ring you've given her. I always think diamonds are the only stones for an engagement-ring. Let me look at it again, Laurie.'

Laurie held up her hand, and Ella inspected the stones that flashed on her finger. Privately, Laurie still felt faintly uncomfortable with it. The diamonds were so large, so dominating on her slender hand, and she would have preferred the smaller solitaire that she had seen on the next tray. But Alec had dismissed her choice, saying that nothing but the best was good enough for his fiancée and, besides, the smaller one was too insignificant. 'I want everyone to know you're mine,' he'd said, and Laurie had given in and agreed to wear the large cluster.

'Yes, very impressive,' Ella said, and again Laurie felt that twinge of discomfort. 'Insignificant'. . . 'impressive'—what did these words have to do with a symbol of love?

They were all surprised by the sound of the doorbell ringing then. Ella stood up to answer it, but Laurie was nearest the door, and her aunt sat down again, smiling. 'It'll be someone who wants to see you anyway, Laurie—everyone's dying to meet Alec and hear all about everything.'

Laurie went to open the front door, wondering which of Aunt Ella's friends had been unable to contain her curiosity any longer. Probably Mary-Jean Sanders, who had to be the first with any piece of news, and would adore having been first to meet the man whose name was fast becoming synonymous with home computers. She turned the knob, a social smile already on her face.

And found herself looking up at a sunburned face. Into eyes of deep cobalt-blue. At thick, waving hair the colour of an autumn sunset. At lips that were firm, unsmiling, yet which she knew could break into a wide, attractive grin. Or had been able to, when he'd been a lanky teenager and she an adoring small girl.

'Russ...' she said faintly, and put her hand out to the door-jamb, as if to hold herself upright.

Russ Brandon—the boy-next-door of her childhood, the boy she had looked up to and hero-worshipped in those days when life had been a game, carefree and filled with laughter, in the days when her parents had been alive... Russ Brandon, twelve years older than she, standing midway in age between her and her father, as much her parents' friend as hers. Russ, who had gone camping with them, helped her with her first fishing-line, held her in the water as she learned to swim, taken her to see an osprey's nest out at the lake...

The dark eyes widened as he looked down at her, the straight brows rising. He looked almost as sur-prised as she was—yet, if he hadn't known she was here, why had he come? She caught at the thought and ran it through her mind ruefully; why should he have come if he *had* known she was here? It was sev-enteen years since he had either seen or heard of her. He must have forgotten all about that skinny little girl who had followed him everywhere out at the lake.

But it seemed that he hadn't forgotten—and, even more amazing, he actually recognised her.

'Laurie,' he said, and his voice was the voice she had known, deeper and more mature, but still Russ's voice. 'By all that's wonderful . . . what are *you* doing here?' He put out his hand, almost as an automatic reaction and, just as automatically, Laurie found herself taking it. It was warm and strong, the long fingers wrapping themselves around hers, and she gasped as she felt her fingers tingle at the contact. She wanted to pull her hand away, but he didn't let go. He went on holding it, his eyes burning her face.

'I—I've come to see my aunt and uncle,' she stuttered. For some reason, she couldn't tell him she'd brought her fiancé to meet them—not straight away. 'Is it so astonishing? It's more surprising that *you're* here—I didn't think your family had any contact with Aunt Ella and Uncle John.'

His face hardened a little. 'No more we do, normally. As a matter of fact, I came to ask for your address.' He looked down at her, frowning. 'Laurie——'

But, before he could say any more, Ella's voice sounded from the living-room. 'Who is it, Laurie? Bring them in—don't keep them standing on the doorstep. They'll want to meet Alec, and help celebrate!'

Russ glanced at the door, then looked back into Laurie's face. His frown had deepened. 'Celebrate?' he said, and Laurie's heart seemed to lurch a little. 'Look, I don't want to intrude——'

'No, you're not intruding.' She found she was still holding his hand, and looked down at it blankly, seeing the strength of the brown fingers as they wound around her own. Suddenly she didn't want him to leave—not just like that. Seventeen years had rolled away, and it was today that was an intrusion, not the past. 'You must come in now.' She turned and went into the room, so that he had to follow, but her mind was in turmoil. Why had he come? Why should he want her address? And what was he going to think of Alec?

She didn't know why that should be important—but somehow it was.

Her aunt and uncle were standing up expectantly as she came in. Alec was still in his armchair, leaning back as if he was entirely at home. Then Russ came slowly through the door. And there was a moment's complete silence.

He glanced from Ella to John, nodded briefly, and held out his hand. 'Mrs Marchant ... Mr Marchant. Good to see you again. Sorry to intrude on a family gathering—I'd no idea. But I won't keep you long. I just came to——' His eyes were on Alec, and he turned his head and looked at Laurie.

Ella Marchant found her voice. 'Russ! Well, what a strange coincidence that you should come here to-night.' She turned to her husband. 'You remember Russ Brandon, don't you? The eldest Brandon boy— they used to live at Kingston, and spent a lot of time out at the lake with my sister. Your father's a lawyer, isn't he?' she added to Russ. Her voice was high and nervous, as if Russ's arrival had stirred up un-welcome memories, and Laurie remembered the pain of her own slow realisation that the Brandons had forgotten her. She glanced quickly at Russ and saw that same unsmiling look on his face, as if he was regretting having come at all. And yet ... there was something in his face, some lurking, half-hidden ex-pression that she couldn't quite pin down, something... He turned his glance upon her, and she caught her breath, feeling a sudden shock like a blow to her heart, and experienced a dizzying sensation, almost as if she was drowning in that blazing cobalt-blue...

'Well,' Alec said out of the mists, 'aren't you going to introduce me, darling? I'm sure you'd like me to know your childhood hero.'

Laurie felt her cheeks colour as she turned to Alec. Her aunt and uncle were watching curiously, but before she could speak John stepped forward and held his hand out to Russ.

'Well, it's good to see you, my boy,' he said heartily. 'It must be—let's see, twenty years or so. You were still in high school. What are you doing now? Weren't you going to follow your father into law?'

'That's right.' Russ's eyes moved again to Laurie before he took John Marchant's hand and shook it. 'I'm a partner now in the firm in Kingston.' Laurie felt her heart kick a little at the mention of her childhood home. 'That's really why I'm here,' Russ went on. 'I wanted to contact Laurie. I'm working in our Ottawa office for a while, and it seemed a good opportunity. I had no idea she'd be here, though.' His eyes were on her again, disturbingly dark, as if he was asking her a question.

'Oh, she and Alec have come to spend a few days with us to celebrate their engagement,' Ella said at once, and Laurie saw Russ's glance drop to her hand. She moved instinctively as if to hide the ring flashing on her finger, then drew back her hand. Why should she want to hide it? She forced herself to listen to her aunt, who was still talking with an odd nervousness in her voice. 'How fortunate that you should drop by just now. You must come to the party we're having tomorrow evening. But I dare say you're too busy.'

Nobody could have mistaken her tone. She was clearly telling Russ to agree that he was too busy, and to decline her invitation. But Laurie, watching the lean, tanned face, saw a muscle tighten in his cheek. Russ Brandon wasn't accustomed to being told what to do, she thought, and was not in the least surprised to hear him say, 'No, I'm not too busy at all, Mrs Marchant. I'll be delighted to come to your party.' He turned to Laurie. 'You still haven't introduced me to your fiancé,' he said politely.

'Oh—I'm sorry.' Flustered, Laurie got to her feet and went to stand beside Alec. 'Alec, this is Russ Brandon, who used to live next door to us in Kingston. Russ, this is my—fiancé, Alec Hadlow. He's managing director of Hadlow Electronics.'

'The computer firm?' Russ said as they shook hands. 'Why, I see your name everywhere! The new Hadlow PC seems to have taken the world of home computing by storm. It eclipses all its predecessors, so I understand.'

'It does indeed.' Alec lifted a hand to smooth back his greying hair. 'I think it will take other manufacturers quite a while to catch up. By which time, of course, we shall have some new innovation. We mean to stay ahead of the game at Hadlow, and I think I can say there's no doubt that we'll do so.'

'How very satisfying for you,' Russ murmured, and turned back to Laurie. 'And are you part of this successful business?'

'No, I'm personnel manager at a fashion house in Toronto,' Laurie answered. 'I've been there for several years now—ever since I left college.' She paused. A hundred questions filled her mind. Russ's appearance had brought back so many memories—memories of the two families, living side by side, the children all older than herself yet always willing to let her join in, to take her on hikes and picnics. She saw again Russ's parents, his mother always ready with a cookie and a kiss, his father so calm and kindly. His two sisters, Cilla and Jane, flitting in and out of the house like butterflies, always laughing. And Russ himself . . .

But she couldn't ask any of the questions. When she had come here after her parents' death, there had been a complete break with the friends of her previous life. She had never really understood why, but her aunt had explained one day that it was inevitable—and probably better. 'You're just a little girl,' she had said kindly. 'Your life is with us now—you can't expect busy people like the Brandons to think about you when you live so far away. And it's not always a good idea to try to hold on to the past. People do change, you know.'

Laurie had tried hard to accept these words. But she had still felt hurt and abandoned by the family she had looked upon almost as her own. And now, looking at Russ's tanned face and brilliant cobalt-blue eyes, she felt a return of that old, forgotten pain.

'How are your mother and father, Russ?' she asked formally. 'And Cilla and Jane—what are they doing?'

'Mum and Dad are about the same—older, that's all.' His eyes were curious as he looked at her, and she felt for a moment as if she were under a microscope. What was he seeing? What was he thinking? 'Cilla—she's married with kids now—two boys, who are holy terrors, and a girl, who's sweet as a peach. And Jane's a financial wizard in one of the city banks.'

His face lightened with a sudden grin. 'You'd never have thought it, would you? She was the biggest scatterbrain of us all!'

They were all sitting down again by now, with fresh drinks, and Laurie was aware of Alec shifting in his seat. She turned to him and smiled.

'I'm sorry, Alec. You know how it is when you meet an old friend—you can't help reminiscing a little. Russ and his brothers and sisters used to take me out with them quite a lot, so of course I have a lot of memories.' But why didn't you ever come to see me here? she wanted to ask. Why didn't you ask me to stay, as your mother promised when I left Kingston?

Those were questions she couldn't ask. But Alec had one of his own.

'Of course, it's fascinating to meet someone from the past,' he agreed, then turned to Russ. 'But you said you came here tonight because you wanted to see Laurie. Why was that, exactly? Did you know she'd be here?'

'Indeed not. As I said, I had no idea—my call tonight was purely fortuitous. No, I simply wanted an address where I could contact her, and Mr and Mrs Marchant seemed the most likely people to know. So, as I was in Ottawa for Canada Day, I thought I'd call in.'

'But why did you want to find me?' Laurie asked. 'After all these years...?' And she could not keep the faint hint of reproach from her voice.

Russ's eyes rested on her thoughtfully. 'It's a legal matter. I had to contact you for the office. There's something——'

'A *legal* matter?' Alec broke in. 'But how can your family firm have anything to do with Laurie's legal affairs? And wouldn't a letter have served the same purpose? Mr Marchant would have been pleased to send on anything that came addressed to Laurie, I'm sure.'

Russ looked at him. 'I'm sure he would. I simply took it into my head to call instead. Laurie was rather more than a client, after all. But if I've caused offence——' He began to rise to his feet.

'Oh, no! Please don't go!' Laurie cried, putting out a hand to stop him. 'Alec didn't mean that at all—did you, Alec? He was just surprised—and he always thinks of doing things in the most efficient way. He'd forgotten we were such friends.'

'I never actually knew,' Alec observed. 'And since you were only seven or eight years old at the time . . . but no matter. No doubt Mr Brandon will tell us what this legal matter is.'

Russ shook his head. 'If Laurie wants to discuss it now, of course I will,' he said, and then spoke directly to her. 'But I think it would be preferable for you to call on me at the firm's office in the city, and we can go through it quietly. I'll have all the papers there—it will be easier to explain. As I say, I didn't expect to find you here this evening, so I didn't bring any documents with me.'

'Documents?' Laurie repeated, bewildered. 'Russ, I don't understand. What documents can you possibly have that are anything to do with me? What's happened?'

This time he looked at John Marchant, sitting silent in his chair, and then at Ella.

'I take it you've not mentioned it to her,' he said, and Laurie, following his glance, saw her uncle's unnatural stillness and her aunt's sudden flush. 'You've not told her that Tom has died?'

'Tom——?' Laurie began, and stared at him as her memory clicked, bringing a picture to the screen of her mind. A tall, thin man, rather older than her father, paddling his canoe into the sunset. His brother, Tom. Her uncle Tom.

She had seen and heard nothing of him since the day when it all happened.

'Uncle Tom's died?' she said uncertainly, and Russ nodded.

'There's a matter of inheritance,' he told her, and this time he did rise to his feet. 'But I can't discuss it now. I have another appointment—I hadn't intended staying even as long as this.' He looked down at Laurie, and she stared back at him, her face so cold that she knew it must be white. 'I'm sorry to have broken it to you like this. It was clumsy of me—but I thought you would probably know.' He allowed his glance, ice-cool, to rest briefly on the faces of John and Ella Marchant. Then he reached into his pocket and drew out a card, which he handed to her. 'That's the address of our Ottawa office. Come and see me the day after tomorrow. Eleven o'clock would be ideal, if that's convenient to you. I'll tell you all about it then.' He turned to leave.

Ella moved forward. Her face was still flushed and there was a perplexed look in her eyes. Her voice was slightly higher than usual as she said, 'But the party, Mr Brandon. Surely you're coming to our party?'

Russ paused at the door. His glance swept over the people in the room: John Marchant, still silent, Alec suspicious, Ella flustered. And Laurie, who knew that she too must look utterly bewildered. He wouldn't come, she thought, and lifted her eyes to his face.

There was a moment of total contact between them. Laurie saw his eyes darken, and felt her heart kick. Her lips parted slightly and she felt suddenly breathless.

'Thank you, Mrs Marchant,' Russ said quietly. 'I'd like to come. I'd like it very much.' He let his eyes maintain contact with Laurie's for a second longer, then he turned and left the room.

There was a pause. Ella hurried out to let him out of the house. Laurie looked down at the carpet. She heard Alec expel a long breath, and waited for him to speak.

'Well!' Ella said, coming back into the room. 'What a strange coincidence—Russ Brandon coming just on your first evening at home. And isn't he a distinguished-looking man—quite different from when he was a boy? Such a bohemian family, I always thought, in spite of the father being a lawyer. But——'

'What did he mean by legal matters—and an inheritance?' Alec demanded, breaking into her nervous chatter. 'Laurie?'

'I've no idea.' Laurie turned to her aunt. 'And I had no idea that Uncle Tom had died either. Why didn't you tell me?' She waited a moment, then added quietly, 'You did know about it, didn't you?'

Ella looked from her to John Marchant, and Laurie realised suddenly that her aunt was actually afraid of her husband. And suddenly, with that realisation, a lot of things shifted slightly and fitted into new places. Memories that had never seemed quite right, but could be explained by this one simple fact. She felt an unexpected pang of pity for her aunt. But she still needed an answer to her question.

She looked at her uncle and saw the closed hardness of his expression. For a moment, she too felt a quiver of fear. Then she reminded herself that her uncle John had never been anything other than kind to her—firm, certainly, unyielding at times, but never harsh or cruel. The idea that she—or anyone—should fear him was ridiculous. She must be over-tired to allow such fantasies into her mind.

'Why didn't you tell me about Uncle Tom?' she asked again, persisting even though she knew that her questions were as unwelcome as Russ's appearance had been. Her uncle and aunt had never encouraged her memories of her life before she had come to live with them. They had never permitted her to talk of the things she had done with her parents; they had tried to help her forget the past, telling her that it was best to start again, to be a daughter to them instead of to Mike and Sue Clive. And, feeling that she owed them that at least, she had tried to bury those memories.

If anyone had asked me, I would have said I'd succeeded, she thought now. But Russ's appearance had undammed a flood of longing for those buried memories. And among them were the memories of her uncle Tom—who had died without her knowing.

'Tell me,' she said with a sudden urgency in her voice. 'You must see you have to tell me now—please.'

'Laurie!' Alec said from his chair. 'You're getting overwrought—there's no need to speak like that. I'm sure your uncle has every intention of telling you. He simply didn't want to upset you, especially at a time like this.'

'A time like——?' She turned to him in surprise, then caught the flash of the ring on her finger. 'Oh—yes.' She looked back at her uncle. 'I'm sorry, Uncle John. I wasn't thinking—of course you were waiting until a better time. But now——'

'Very well. There's little to tell after all.' John Marchant spoke without really looking at her. 'Your uncle Tom had been ill for some time. He lived alone, as you know, at that cottage he had out on the lake, and wouldn't move back to town as his friends wanted him to. He could manage to look after himself, after a fashion, and did so until the end. He was found three weeks ago, dead in the boat he used for fishing. That's all.'

'That's *all*?' Laurie stared at him, her imagination adding flesh to the bones of the story she had just heard. 'You mean he was all by himself, until the very end? He had nobody—nobody at all?'

'It was the way he wanted it,' John said. 'And who should he have, after all? He had no relatives.'

'He did have a relative,' Laurie reminded him, and her voice was tight with tears. 'He had me. His niece. *I* was a relative.'

'But Laurie,' her aunt said, 'you had no contact with him for nearly twenty years.'

'I know,' Laurie said, and she stood up and looked from one to the other. 'And whose fault was that?'

Keeping her head high for fear of the tears falling from her eyes, she turned and left the room. She went upstairs to the bedroom she had slept in as a child, went in, and closed the door behind her. She leaned against it, still struggling with the tears. She must not let them fall. She must not cry. She must do anything rather than cry.

She walked to the bed and sank down on it, still taut with the effort she was making; then she bowed her head. Why not let them come? Why shouldn't she grieve for her uncle as she had never been allowed to grieve for her father and mother? Why did it have to be so wrong to give way to emotion?

But when she tried to let the tears fall, she found that they had dried in her eyes. And, although she lay down and buried her head in her arms, they refused to come, to ease the ache of grief that throbbed through her body. And she knew that she needed them.

Later on, Alec came and knocked on her door. His tone was first coaxing, as if he were talking to a naughty child, then exasperated. But Laurie did not answer him and eventually he went away. She rolled over on to her back and stared up at the ceiling.

Why hadn't she been able to respond to him? Surely she ought to have been able to find comfort in the arms of her future husband, if in no other way? But it wasn't Alec she was thinking of now. It wasn't his comfort she longed for.

It was another face that she saw in her mind. A face she had known well when she was a small child. A face she had run to when she had hurt herself, when she had some small pleasure or triumph to communicate, whenever she'd needed a friend. A lean, tanned face with cobalt-blue eyes.

Why had Russ Brandon come here tonight, of all nights? Why did he want to see her? And what 'inheritance' had her uncle Tom left her?

Laurie had the sensation that she was standing on the brink of some kind of cliff. Below and before her stretched the future, unknown and frightening. She shivered.

She had expected that, once she was engaged to Alec, there would be nothing more to make her afraid. It seemed she had been wrong.

CHAPTER TWO

'IT ALL looks very beautiful, Laurie. And so do you.'

Laurie leaned against the wall and looked down into the champagne glass in her hand. The noise of the party ebbed and flowed around her. She thought of all the people she had met and talked with, the hands she had shaken, the cheeks she had kissed, all no more than a blur. She wanted nothing more than to run away from them all, to hide herself somewhere until she had time to come to terms with her new life. It was all happening too quickly.

It was all Russ Brandon's fault, disorientating her as he had by calling so unexpectedly and bringing back memories that were better forgotten. Bringing the news of her uncle, with the guilt that she had never visited him. But John and Ella were right. It had been better for her to make a clean break with her former life, to grow up in their mould, and it was better to keep it that way now.

Russ Brandon had no relevance to her life now. And once she had found out just what this inheritance was, and collected it from his office, he would drop out of it as if he had never been.

But for now he was here, watching her as she swirled the champagne in her glass, and telling her she was beautiful. Laurie made an effort and looked up into his cobalt eyes.

'Thank you. And I'm glad you could come. It's good to meet old friends.'

'I notice I'm the only one from Kingston,' he observed. 'The only one who knew your parents, I would think. I wonder why that is.'

'My aunt and uncle had a different circle of friends. There's no more to it than that. Kingston's quite a long way away, after all—it's unlikely they'd have known the same people.'

'But I thought this party was for *your* friends too,' he said quietly.

Laurie looked down into her glass again. 'It is. These people are my friends.'

'And those from Kingston aren't?'

'I lost touch with them all—I was only eight years old——'

'But we would have liked to keep in touch. My mother missed you—you were special to her. She wanted you to come and stay.'

Laurie lifted her head sharply. 'I never knew that.'

'Didn't you?' His eyes were on hers, holding her glance. 'Didn't you really? Or did you just prefer your new life—the pleasures of the city, the new friends you made, the comfortable life your uncle and aunt could offer you?' He glanced around the room with its too opulent furnishings. 'Your father and mother didn't have much money,' he said quietly. 'They couldn't give you much in the way of clothes or fancy toys. But they gave you a lot of fun, doing simple things like camping and hiking and canoeing. And they gave you a lot of love.'

Laurie's eyes misted with tears. 'I know. I know that. I never forgot——'

'No?' he said, and his voice was cool. 'So why did you neglect your father's brother? Why did you let poor Tom die without ever seeing you again—his only relative?'

Pain sliced through Laurie's heart, and she cried out again, 'I was only eight years old! How could I——?'

'It's a long time,' Russ Brandon said coldly, 'since you were eight years old.' He turned away and placed his glass on a small table. 'I'm sorry. I have to go now. But I'll see you in the morning, in the office. You have the address, I believe?' He nodded as if to a stranger. 'Until tomorrow, then, Laurie. And—enjoy your party.'

He took a few swift strides to the door, and vanished. And Laurie looked after him and felt a cold loneliness touch her heart.

Enjoy her party? *Her* party? Once again, she had the strange feeling that none of this had anything at all to do with her. And she recalled the conversation she and Alec had had yesterday.

'Ottawa, on Canada Day,' Alec had pronounced as the big car drew smoothly nearer to the city, 'is really nothing more than a rather vulgar party.'

Laurie looked at him doubtfully. 'Vulgar?' There was a touch of dismay in her voice. 'I've always thought it was rather fun. Going to hear the speeches from Parliament House, seeing the celebrities, singing "Oh, Canada" . . . it's always given me a thrill.'

'Oh, that part's all right,' Alec conceded, increasing speed to pass a truck. 'Any good patriotic Canadian would appreciate that. You're quite right to feel emotional about it, darling.' He gave her an approving smile. 'But the rest of it—all the junketing around the city, the side-shows and entertainments, the noise and jostling—you can't enjoy *that*, I'm sure.'

Laurie hesitated. Part of her wanted to say that yes, she did enjoy it. She loved wandering around the city, which looked so different from its everyday self, with the roads free of traffic, the streets gay with flags and bunting. She loved stopping to watch a clown or juggler, browsing around the various displays and laughing at the costumes some people wore. Most of all, she loved the evening, with its tremendous firework display filling the sky with brilliant colour and rocking the ground beneath her feet with its explosions.

She brushed back her long, almost blue-black hair, and opened her mouth to explain this, but before she could begin Alec was speaking again, his tone kindly, as if explaining something to a small child.

'Of course, you haven't actually been in Ottawa for Canada Day for quite a long time, have you? You must have been quite young—no more than a teenager—when you were last here on July the First. Naturally, you would have enjoyed it then.' He smiled, his glance moving approvingly over Laurie's smart linen suit and smooth hair. 'You're rather more sophisticated now. Though I'm surprised that your aunt and uncle allowed you to go about on your own. From what you've told me about them, it's always struck me that they were exceptionally careful with you.'

'They were.' Laurie remembered her pleas to be allowed to go into the city with her friends, and Aunt Ella's reluctance to agree. 'I went without telling them,' she confessed with a rueful grin. 'I said I was spending the day with a friend, and we went together. I was terrified someone would see me and tell them— they would have been so angry.'

'I should think so too!' Alec's small mouth pursed. 'And I'm surprised that you should have been so deceitful, Laurie. It's not what I would have expected.'

Laurie felt a twinge of irritation. 'Well, there's no need to take it so seriously, Alec. I was only fourteen — young girls do that sort of thing sometimes. I never deceived them in any other way — but I *did* want to go and see everything. And the next year I went quite openly.'

'All the same . . .' Alec shook his head. 'Oh, well, as you say, it's a long time ago now. It wouldn't be fair to hold a sin committed eleven years ago against you. And I'm sure you wouldn't dream of doing anything like that now.'

Laurie looked at him, her green eyes clouded. She didn't know quite what to say. Her childish deceit seemed to have taken on proportions it had never warranted, even at the time. All she had done was go to Kelly's house and then into the city with her friend and the girl's parents and brother. They had wandered about all day, enjoying the sights, gone back again in the evening for the fireworks, and next day she had returned home.

'I'm looking forward to meeting your uncle and aunt,' Alec observed. 'You were lucky to have relatives like them to take you in, Laurie.'

'Yes, I was.' She wondered why her voice didn't sound more enthusiastic. She loved her aunt Ella and uncle John — of course she did. Hadn't they given her a home when her parents had died together in that terrible accident? Hadn't they looked after her and brought her up as if she were their own daughter? Hadn't they made every effort to ensure that she grew up with the principles they had always lived by, the firm ethics that Uncle John said were disappearing everywhere?

And they had succeeded—so much so that she felt slightly out of tune with most of the people of her own generation, who seemed to think of nothing but enjoying their lives. Indeed, it wasn't until she had met Alec that she had thought there was any chance of love and marriage for her—but in Alec she had found a second Uncle John, smoothly confident and self-assured, with a rigid code of ethics that gave her a sense of safety. Keep within these rules, she could hear her uncle saying, and nothing can go wrong. You will always be in the right.

It was important for Laurie to feel herself supported by a code of rules. Until she was eight years old, her life in Kingston, Ontario, had been unstructured, her parents carefree and adventurous. Weekends were always an event—Laurie never knew in advance what was likely to happen. A weekend on the lake, at the cottage they'd built with their own hands before she was born; a day learning to hang-glide, with Laurie watching, half terrified, half excited, on the ground; a few days' skiing when the snow had fallen; swimming, fishing, camping. And then— the end of it all.

She turned abruptly and watched the city of Ottawa come closer, feeling almost as if she were a child again, seeking comfort and safety. She looked at Alec again. She knew her aunt and uncle would approve of him. He was exactly their kind of person. Exactly the kind of man to give her what they had taught her to expect, even to need.

So why, just at that moment, did the picture of a small pigtailed girl, tagging along after a tall, sunburned boy, flit through her mind?

The Canada Day celebrations were over and the city being cleaned of the last remaining debris as Laurie made her way to Russ Brandon's office to keep their appointment. She felt a sense of having missed something important as she looked at the expanse of grass in front of Parliament House, and thought of the crowds that would have collected there yesterday to hear the Governor's speech and sing the national song. The displays, too—showing Canada's past heritage and extolling her present and future, with each ethnic group represented in song, dance, craft and skill to celebrate their unity as Canadians—she regretted not having seen them. And the grand firework display in the evening, with rockets bursting into a great kaleidoscope of colour behind and around the great clock-tower of Parliament House and over the river— if only she could have been here to see them, rather than at the party where she had felt so false.

Laurie looked up at the tall building, where she had come to meet Russ Brandon. Its glass sides glittered in the July sun. His family firm must have done well, to have offices in Ottawa as well as in Kingston. And Russ had had all the confident aura of a successful man. It was difficult to realise that he had once been the lanky youth she remembered from her childhood.

Inside the building, she was directed to the fifteenth floor. And as the lift door slid open she walked out almost into Russ's arms.

'Oh—I hadn't realised——'

'Reception rang to tell me you were on your way.'
He looked unsmilingly at her, and she remembered
the coolness with which they had parted last night.
'Well, how did the party go? I wondered whether you
might be able to make an eleven o'clock appointment. Thought you might still be in bed——'

'Sleeping it off?' she took him up quickly. 'No,
Russ—as you see, I'm perfectly wide awake and even
able to talk intelligently.'

He grinned slightly and led her into one of the
offices leading off the corridor. It was light and airy,
with a large desk near the big window. Laurie took a
few steps towards it, then stopped.

'What a fantastic view!'

She felt Russ come to stand close behind her, and
the hairs prickled on the nape of her neck.

'It's pretty good, isn't it? The whole of Ottawa at
your feet. Parliament buildings on the skyline, the
river curving round below them, shimmering in the
sun—yes, it's pretty spectacular.'

'Well, you needn't talk as if you'd invented it
yourself,' Laurie said drily, moving away from him.
She glanced around the office. 'You certainly seem to
have done well. I congratulate you.'

'Well, we work hard and we do our best by our
clients.' He moved over to a small corner table where
a coffee-maker bubbled gently. 'Can I offer you a
coffee?'

'Thank you.' Laurie sat down in one of the
comfortable chairs facing the desk, but Russ shook
his head and motioned her to the armchairs and sofa
which made a small group facing the window.

'Sit over there—we'll enjoy the view as we drink our coffee. We've got a lot to catch up on, Laurie. As we were saying last night—it's been a long time.'

Feeling that she would have preferred to keep this meeting formal, Laurie moved over to an easy chair. She accepted a cup and gazed out at the gleaming city around and below her.

'Ottawa is always beautiful, isn't it?' she said softly. 'As it is now, glittering in the summer sun—the whole city seems to be made of glass, doesn't it? And in winter, when everything sparkles with snow and the river's frozen and filled with people skating to work. I've always loved it.'

'Yet you live in Toronto,' he pointed out, and Laurie smiled a little ruefully.

'I went there for my work, and I'll stay because it's where Alec has his headquarters. We'll make our home there. Toronto's a beautiful city too,' she added a little defensively.

'And Kingston? You'd never go back there?'

'Kingston belongs to the past,' she said, and was aware of the tightness in her voice.

Russ looked at her for a moment. Then he set down his cup and leaned slightly towards her. Laurie felt her heart thump. His face was close to hers, the dark eyes compelling, the mouth firm yet questioning. She felt the faint touch of his breath against her cheek, and as she saw his gaze drop to her mouth she felt her lips part, and ran her tongue nervously over them. Her hand shook and the coffee-cup rattled slightly in its saucer. Without taking his eyes from her face, Russ took the cup and saucer from her unresisting fingers and set it on the table. His hand brushed her cheek, very lightly, and she felt a tingle as his fingers touched her skin.

'Are you sure of that, Laurie? Are you quite sure?' His voice was deep, little more than the purr of a cat, and for a moment she could not think what he meant. Something about Kingston ... the past ... She shook her head, trying to think clearly through the mist, and Russ moved away from her.

They looked at each other, gravely, searchingly, as if there was a question between them that must be answered. Then Laurie said, 'Perhaps you should tell me why I'm here, Russ. You must be very busy—I don't want to hold you up.' She stood up and moved back towards the desk. 'I can't imagine it's anything very important, anyway.'

'That depends on what you consider important.' He followed her and stood on the other side of the desk, facing her. His eyes were shadowed, sombre, with no trace of a smile. 'Admittedly, an old man's dying wish can't be set against the affairs of a successful businessman and his executive fiancée——'

'I didn't mean that!' Indignation brought tears unexpectedly to her throat. 'I mean it couldn't be important for *you*.' She looked around the office, gestured helplessly. 'You obviously have a lot of rich and important clients—whatever you get from administering Uncle Tom's estate must be peanuts——'

'Tom was a friend,' Russ said tersely. 'There are some things you don't do for money, Laurie. Or have you forgotten that, living your busy life in Toronto?'

Laurie stared at him. She was aware of her body shaking. She raised a trembling hand to push back the dark hair that hung over her forehead. 'Of course I haven't forgotten it. What do you take me for, Russ?'

His eyes swept over her, taking in her smooth hair, her impeccably made-up complexion, her plain, expensive suit and shoes. She saw his gaze linger on the ring that flashed on her finger, the ring that proclaimed her as Alec's. She felt the colour flood into her cheeks.

'I think you're right,' Russ said after a pause. 'It would be better if we got down to business. Sit down, please, Laurie. We may as well discuss this in a civilised fashion.'

Laurie bit back a retort, and sat down, feeling somewhat like a child summoned to the presence of the headmaster. She waited as Russ searched for a file and opened it, glancing quickly through the contents.

'Well?' she demanded at last. 'What is it all about, Russ? Just what has Uncle Tom left me in his will? It can't have been much—he had nothing—unless he made a lot of money in the last few years of his life, which I doubt.'

'I'd doubt it too,' Russ said drily. 'There was never anyone less interested in making money than Tom. Living at the lake, messing about in his old boat, and doing a spot of fishing—that was all Tom was ever really interested in.' He glanced up suddenly and their eyes met across the wide desk. 'I've never known anyone so in tune with nature as he was,' he remarked quietly. 'He seemed to be a part of all that, out on the lake. The weather, the seasons—Tom was in harmony with them all. He knew the movements of every bird and animal. The loons, the ospreys, the beavers—they were his friends.'

Laurie was silent. Russ's words had brought back pictures to her mind. Pictures of the lake where she and her parents and her uncle Tom had spent weekends. Pictures of herself, paddling a canoe with her uncle at dusk as they watched the banks of the islands for a beaver to appear. Pictures of herself with her father, walking into the water and peering down at the fish nests close to their toes.

She looked down at her fingers, laced tightly in her lap, and realised that her eyes were misted with tears. One dropped on to her hand, and she moved quickly, covering it with her fingers, anxious that Russ should not see her moment of weakness. But when she glanced up again he had turned back to the file.

'Tell me,' she said, and her voice was soft. 'Tell me about Uncle Tom. I ought to have gone to see him during all those years. Tell me about him now.'

'Don't you want to know what he's left you?' Russ asked, and she shook her head.

'I want to know about him.'

Russ looked at her, and for the first time she detected a glimmer of warmth in his eyes.

'All the same,' he said, 'I think you should know just what it is he's left you—and what the conditions are.'

'Conditions?'

'Yes,' he confirmed, 'there are conditions. Whether you choose to fulfil them is, of course, for you to decide. You may not want to.'

'Tell me.'

Russ looked once more at the file, then closed it, leaned back in his chair, and gazed steadily into her eyes. Laurie found that her heart was beating quickly. She met his gaze squarely, her chin lifting a little.

'Your uncle Tom always wanted to see you again,' he began slowly. 'He lived for news of you—and he didn't get much. But he managed to follow your career, through school and college. He was proud of you when you began to do well in your job. But he longed—always—for more contact with you. And I know his greatest wish was that you should go back to Kingston some day, go out to the lake and be as you were when you were a child, so full of enthusiasm, so interested in everything.' The cobalt eyes hardened a little. 'I used to curse you for not being there sometimes,' Russ said with a note of anger running like steel through his voice. 'I wanted to go and get you, fetch you back to show you a man who loved you and longed for your love. But he wouldn't allow it. You had to come of your own free will, because you wanted to, or it would be meaningless.'

Laurie stared at Russ through a curtain of tears that she made no effort now to hide. The thought of her uncle, lonely and longing for her, his only relative, was like a pain in her heart. How could she have been so thoughtless, so cruel?

'But I didn't know,' she whispered. 'I never heard from him—just a card at Christmas and on my birthday. I didn't know he wanted to see me.'

'He wrote,' Russ told her, 'often. You never answered.'

Her lips were dry, the words little more than a breath of sound as she realised what must have happened.

'I never had his letters.'

There was a silence as she grappled with the truth. Her aunt's and uncle's disapproval of her parents and their way of life. Their insistence that a 'clean break' was best for the child so cruelly orphaned. Their strict discipline, so different from the carefree way of life

she had known. The letters—from how many
people?—she had never received.

'Tell me,' she said at last. 'Tell me what he left.
And what the conditions are.'

Russ leaned forward again. He rested his hands on
the desk and she looked at the long fingers.

'Tom left you all he had,' Russ said quietly. 'His
boat and his cottage at the lake. Everything.'

'His . . . cottage?'

'It was your cottage once,' Russ reminded her.
'Your father and mother built that cottage themselves. You spent your holidays in it. When they died,
John Marchant decided it should be sold and the
money used for your upbringing. Tom scraped
together every penny he had, and bought it.' He
paused. 'I take it you never knew that either?'

Laurie shook her head. 'I had no idea. And now
he's left it to me?'

'He thought it should have been yours all along.'

'And the conditions?' she asked after a moment.

'He wanted you to live in it. For at least three
months. After that you can sell it, if you want to. But
he wanted you to know the lake again before you decided to do that. He wanted you to recapture your
childhood a little, to understand just what it was that
drew your parents there. To understand their values.'

'And if I don't live in it?'

'His instructions are that the cottage should be sold
and the money given away.' Russ gave her a con-
sidering look. 'I should tell you, Laurie, that you
could contest these conditions and would possibly win
your case. But—that's what Tom wanted.'

'Is there a time limit on this?' she asked, frowning
a little, and Russ grinned sardonically.

'Wondering what the fiancé will say? Do you think he's going to object to his wife-to-be living in an isolated cottage for three months? Or were you planning to spend your honeymoon there together? I don't see it as Alec Hadlow's scene, somehow.'

Laurie felt a flash of annoyance, but she couldn't deny the truth of his words. Alec wasn't likely to look favourably on the idea of living in a lake cottage for three months—nor would he approve of the idea of her staying there alone. Particularly after they were married.

'I don't see how I can do it,' she said at last. 'Alec certainly won't have time to stay there—and neither will I. I have a job, Russ, and a wedding to plan. All in Toronto. How can I set everything aside to spend three months doing nothing miles away from all that? It's just not possible.'

Russ nodded as if he'd expected this. 'I thought you'd say that. In fact, I'd have been very surprised indeed if you'd agreed. Well—that's that, then. I take it you'll want to contest the will. I can't act for you myself, of course, since I represent Tom's estate, but I can give you the name of——'

'Wait!' Laurie felt a pang of distress. 'Russ, I don't want to get caught up in a lot of legal argument——'

'You're willing to give up all title to the estate, then?' He had moved over to his desk and begun to sort out the documents that lay there. 'It's one or the other, Laurie.'

She hesitated, feeling helpless. 'No—but——'

Russ's expression hardened. 'Tom thought this out carefully, Laurie. He had his reasons—good ones too, in my opinion, though now that I've met you again I feel he was being a trifle over-optimistic. But——'

'What do you mean?' She stared at him. 'Russ, what are you saying?'

'I'm saying that you've changed, Laurie. Oh, your uncle wasn't a fool—he knew you'd have been influenced by the Marchants. But he thought you'd still be the same Laurie underneath, still the same eager child, ready to try anything, ready to laugh and live the simple life. I think he was wrong. I think that Laurie has gone, or been so deeply buried that she'll never find her way out again.' His glance travelled over her body, taking in the smart suit, the gleaming hair. 'You're a city girl now, Laurie. You're into materialism. The simple life won't do for you any more.' And the contempt surfaced in his voice at last, killing all the communication there had been between them.

Laurie felt tears sting her eyes, but the pain was quickly overshadowed by her anger. She came to her feet, brushing the betraying wetness from her cheeks, and faced him.

'*I'm* into materialism? And what about you, Russ Brandon? What about all this?' She waved a hand around her, taking in the comfortably furnished office, the great window overlooking the glittering city, the symbols of success. 'You're not concerned with money, are you? You're not working for the rich who can afford your high charges, rather than the poor who can't? There's nothing in the least materialistic about you, is there? Or is that different in some mysterious way? Perhaps you'd like to explain it to me some time.'

Russ looked at her. His mouth tightened and twitched. He waited a moment until she had panted herself into silence.

'I'll explain it to you any time you like to make an appointment,' he said coolly. 'But, as you so rightly surmise, my time is expensive, and I have another appointment at twelve.' He glanced at his watch. 'You asked if there was a time limit on Tom's condition. There is. You can have three months to decide. After that, the cottage will be sold and the proceeds given to charity, as I told you. Perhaps you'd like to let me know some time what your final decision is. Though I doubt——' his eyes moved over her again, resting for a moment on the ring that sparkled on her finger '—whether you'll change your mind. You clearly have much more important things to do with your time.'

Laurie held herself rigidly still, determined not to react to his subtly contemptuous tones. The ring felt like a ton weight. After a moment, she picked up her bag and turned towards the door.

'I'll do that,' she said coolly, thankful that she had regained enough control to keep her voice steady. 'I'll let you know definitely what my decision is as soon as I've talked it over with Alec.'

She left the office without looking at him, and made her way back to her aunt's house, certain that she had done the right thing, certain that Alec would agree.

How could she possibly take three months to stay at the lake? It was a crazy condition.

So why did she feel this hankering to go there again—to revisit the scenes of her childhood, to recapture the magic of those long, carefree days?

Why did she feel that she'd like to take that contempt out of Russ Brandon's eyes and voice?

CHAPTER THREE

'You're going to *live* there?' Alec shook his head, unable to take his eyes from her face. 'Laurie, you're not serious. This is just some silly joke.'

'It isn't at all.' She lifted her chin, irritated. 'It's the condition Uncle Tom laid down, you know that.'

'Yes, but we all know just how that would stand up in a court of law. It's not as if there were any other relatives to contest the will, Laurie—you're the only one. Nobody's going to fight you over this.'

'Russ would.'

'Russ Brandon has no stake at all in this matter. He's not related, merely the old man's lawyer. It's none of his business.'

'All the same——'

'I tell you, Laurie,' Alec said, taking her hand and gripping it in his fingers, 'that cottage is yours. Keep it for a year and no one is going to dispute your right to it. If you're that worried, move a few personal possessions into it, and we'll spend the odd weekend there—though nobody would get me to stay there any longer than a few days. What people find to do in such a benighted spot...' He shook his head again. 'Anyway, it doesn't matter. It'll take us that long to get everything fixed up, so there's no hurry.'

'Get everything fixed up? What do you mean?'

'Why, the plans, all the necessary permissions and so on. There are formalities to be gone through, you know. And there's finance—it's a big project, we'll

41

need backing. I'll have to negotiate that on the best terms—it all takes time.'

Laurie had the feeling that she was on a fast train rushing towards some unknown destination. 'But Alec, we can't do anything until the cottage is really mine. And it won't be, not until——'

'I know,' he interrupted, smiling as if he were a father indulging a petted daughter, 'until you've lived in it for three months. But I've already told you what to do about that. Now, look, I've been working out some figures, and I think——'

'Alec,' she said, cutting into his talk, 'wait a minute. I meant what I said. I do mean to live in the cottage. And I told Russ I would, this morning.'

Alec looked at her in exasperation. 'Laurie, stop being silly——'

'I'm not being silly.'

'You can't possibly mean to live out there, all alone, for three months. What about your job—are you going to throw that up? Jobs as personnel managers in prestigious fashion houses don't fall off trees.'

'I'll take special leave. I've already spoken to Sam Jackson, and he agrees I'm entitled to it. I've had almost no leave since I started there.'

'You've spoken to Jackson? Without consulting me?'

'We're not married yet, Alec,' Laurie reminded him quietly.

'Nevertheless——'

'Alec,' she said, 'I want to do this. It's important to me. Not just because of the inheritance. Because it means something to me, that cottage. My parents built it, and I spent a lot of time there with them. Seeing it again the other week—it made me realise I'd been missing something. I need to make up for what I've missed—and living out there might help me do that. It might help me to come to terms with the past.'

Alec stared at her, clearly baffled by her words.

'But I've already told you, Laurie, we could go out and spend the weekend there. Take some friends with us. We can make some alterations, have an extension built, add a new bedroom and a better bathroom. I don't mind doing any of that—it will all add to the value of the place. And——'

'But we can't do any of that until I've *lived* in it.'

Alec sighed. 'We're going around in circles here. Laurie, you can't just throw up everything and go and live out there for three months. It isn't your job, it's us—my life and work. I have to be in Toronto. I can't have you stuck out on a lake a hundred miles away——'

'Why not?' And before she had even thought what she was going to say, she added, 'You could come and live there with me.'

Even before he answered, she knew that he wouldn't. He would never dream of committing himself to three months' near-solitude on the shore of a lonely lake. He would never leave his business, even in the capable hands of his managers and advisers. He would never understand the pull that the lake exerted on her now.

Not in the way that Russ would. But Russ had changed too. And she remembered the hard look in his eyes as he'd watched her that morning, and felt a sharp twinge of pain.

'You're just being foolish now,' Alec said shortly, as if the indulgent father was losing patience at last.

'I see little point in continuing this conversation if you're simply going to be flippant.'

Flippant? Was *that* what he called it? The pain hardened into a knot of anger. Didn't her wishes count for anything? Was this what it was going to be like all their lives—with Alec treating her as a child whenever she wanted to express her own personality? Belittling the things that were important to her—dismissing her needs as 'silly' or 'flippant'?

'All right,' she said quietly, 'we won't talk about it any more. Just accept that I mean to go and live there, Alec, whatever you say. It's important to me.'

He stared at her, his eyes cold, his small mouth thin and hard.

'In that case,' he said, 'we had better postpone any talk of wedding plans until you come home. You clearly need to get this madness out of your system.'

Laurie looked at him. She looked at the smooth, pale face, the light eyes, the petulant mouth, and wondered what she had ever seen in him. What had she thought he could offer her? What had she wanted to give him?

Love, she thought sadly. That was what she had wanted to offer him. The love that had ached inside her since childhood, the love her aunt and uncle had never seemed to require. Good behaviour was all they had wanted. And she had so much, so much more to give.

But it hadn't been love that they wanted—and now she was beginning to wonder whether Alec wanted it. He wanted a wife he could be proud of, a hostess to entertain his business colleagues, a mother for his children. And in return he had offered her safety. A world where she could live without fear of being hurt.

But—love?

And, unbidden, another face slid into her thoughts. Another man. Laurie thought of Russ Brandon, his lean, hard looks, his searing blue eyes, and shivered. Russ Brandon would offer no safe harbour, she was sure, no haven where one could live without fear of being hurt. His world would be a world where people met pain with courage and did not hide behind the fences they had erected to protect themselves from reality.

But Russ Brandon's world was not hers. And neither, she knew now, was Alec's.

He was watching her now, clearly expecting her to capitulate. But Laurie knew that this was something she must not do. Instead, she touched her engagement-ring, feeling the roughness of the cluster of precious stones, and then, slowly, drew it from her finger and held it out to him.

'I'm sorry, Alec. I don't think it's fair to you for me to go on wearing this. I'm not the person you thought I was—and I'll be different again when I come back from the lake. You ought to be free.'

Alec looked down at the ring, then raised his eyes to meet hers. He looked incredulous.

'You don't mean this, Laurie. You're overwrought. Coming back here, hearing about your uncle, the cottage—it's all been too much for you——'

'Yes, it probably has,' Laurie said thoughtfully. 'It's knocked me sideways a bit. But it's made me think, too.'

'And what have you thought?' His tone was faintly scornful, as if thinking were an activity like piloting a jet aircraft—something Laurie could never expect to achieve.

'Not a lot so far,' she replied honestly. 'In fact, I feel thoroughly confused. But I know I *need* to think—and that's what I mean to do at the cottage. Perhaps after three months there, away from everything else, I'll begin to find out just who I am.'

Alec stared at her, baffled. 'I don't know what you're talking about. ''Find out who you are...?'' It's beyond me. But——' he looked again at the ring '—there's no need to go this far, Laurie. All right, have your three months—though I'll be surprised if you stand it for three weeks—and then come back and we'll talk again. But keep this——' he tried to put the ring back on to her finger '—you and I have a future together. Don't throw that away.'

She tried to resist him, but in the end she agreed to keep the ring—though she refused to put it back on her finger. 'I don't want either of us to feel tied during this time, Alec. After three months, I'll either put it back on, or give it back to you for good.' Privately, she doubted whether she would ever put it back on again. Its bright opulence looked garish and ostentatious. But she was too tired to argue any more, and with that Alec seemed content. He gave her a complacent kiss.

'Off to bed now, my dear. Your uncle didn't really like leaving us alone down here, I could see that, even though I'm sure he could see I'm to be trusted. You know, you'll never have that worry with me—other women, I mean. One's enough for me.' He laughed and gave her a pat on the shoulder as he urged her towards the door.

One might even be too much, Laurie thought as she made her way up the stairs. Alec had never done any more than give her an affectionate kiss—perhaps if he had, if he had shown a more urgent desire, she would have found it more difficult to break their engagement. If he had ever expressed real love . . .

Love. Was she never to know real, honest, urgent love? Or was it something that was only talked and written about? Was it really no more than a myth?

Closing the mesh screen-door behind her, to keep mosquitoes out, Laurie crossed the big single room that was living-room and kitchen in one, and went up the six steps that led to the bedrooms. She hesitated slightly, half inclined to use the small bedroom, with its bunks fixed solidly to the walls, that had been hers as a child. Then she turned the other way and went into the big room her parents and, more recently, her uncle Tom, had used, with the double bed still covered by the patchwork quilt her mother had made. She remembered watching the busy fingers, helping to fold the fabric over the cards, and a lump came into her throat.

The pain was still there, after all these years. Was it too much to ask that Alec should have understood that? And, as she slowly undressed and climbed into the big bed, turning out the lamp so that only moonlight slid into the room, she thought of the day when she had brought him to see her inheritance.

'Well, it's certainly remote enough.' The car had bumped slowly along the unmade track through thick woods. On either side, bushes trailed long fronds across their path, and Laurie heard Alec mutter as they rubbed against the sides of the car. She hoped it wasn't getting scratched.

'I'd forgotten it was so narrow. Everything seems bigger to a child—except our car.' She smiled, thinking of the little runabout they had crammed into for their weekend jaunts. It had been filled with baskets, rugs and other necessities—they had never quite managed to acquire a complete set of equipment for the cottage, so always had to take a lot from home. Sometimes there had barely been room for Laurie in the back seat, and she had been fitted in first, then everything packed around her. When she got out, there was a 'Laurie-shaped' space left behind among the tightly wedged luggage.

'Are you quite sure this is the right way? It looks to me as if it's a dead end.' Alec's voice was tight, as if he was trying hard not to let irritation get the better of him. Laurie put her hand on his knee.

'It's all right. We're nearly there. We take the right fork here, see? Then down into the valley, and we should be able to see . . .' She leaned forward eagerly.

'I don't know how you can be so sure, after such a long time. And how your uncle could have expected you to *live* in such a benighted place——' Alec slammed on the brakes and swore as an animal ran across in front of the car. 'What was that?'

'A racoon. You must know what a racoon looks like. The woods are full of animals, Alec.'

'Hmm.' His grunt suggested that this was another thing that would have to be changed if the firm was to use the cottage for senior executives. 'I hope it's safe.'

'As safe as any other part of the country.' Laurie kept her own tone in check. She was alarmed by the irritation Alec's attitude was causing her—and it was more than irritation, too. A kind of fear . . . Yet was it so important that they agree on everything? Shouldn't a secure relationship be able to accept some differences of opinion?

The car juddered over the last part of the track and arrived at a turning point. Alec swung it carefully to the right and they found themselves looking down through a cleared space, with just a few graceful trees left standing. Beyond them stood a large wood-built cabin, raised up above the ground with a porch running around three sides. And beyond that lay the shimmering waters of the lake.

The sound of the car's engine faded, and there was silence. But it wasn't silence at all, Laurie realised a moment later. The air was filled with sound—the sound of birdsong, of air moving gently in the leaves, of water lapping softly on the beach. She could hear bees on the flowers of a bush near by, the rustle of some small animal in the undergrowth. She could almost hear the sound of a bird's feet walking across the grass.

Laurie sat silent, unable to speak. She let her eyes move over the scene, taking everything in. She felt its peace steal slowly, softly over her, a peace she had forgotten about, a peace she needed. She drew a deep breath.

'Well, so this is the famous cottage,' Alec declared loudly, and his voice was an intrusion in the quiet air. 'Hmm... It doesn't look too bad. Let's go and see.'

He got out of the car and slammed the door behind him. The noise reverberated through Laurie's head. She sat still for a few moments, trying to recapture the sense of peace she had felt, then got out and followed him slowly, closing the door with no more than a soft click.

Alec walked around the cottage, looking at it critically. Laurie walked up the steps on to the porch and moved slowly to the front. She stood quite still, her hands on the wooden balustrade, looking down towards the lake. And, for a second, time split away and shifted, and she was a seven-year-old child again, and her mother and father were coming up the beach, their arms wound around each other's waists, laughing. They couldn't have been much older than I am now, Laurie thought with a sudden shock. Twenty-eight and thirty. And the tragedy of their deaths was like a kick, so that she gasped suddenly and felt the tears hot in her eyes.

This was the memory her uncle and aunt had tried to eradicate, the pain they had tried to save her from. But I ought to experience it, she thought. It's only right that I should.

And, as if that memory had opened the way, others came flooding through her mind. Memories of the Brandon family—Russ, his dark auburn hair flopping over his eyes, his long limbs sunburnt to a deep mahogany, wearing nothing but a pair of old shorts as he sailed the old dinghy or paddled the canoe, his strong hands holding her wriggling body as he taught her to swim, his bright blue eyes laughing as he teased her with a crab, threatening to drop it on her bare tummy as she lay on the sand . . .

His family had been there too—his parents, his brothers, his sisters. But it was Russ she remembered, Russ who dominated her thoughts.

And then time slipped back again, but she knew that the memories would return. She had never really been allowed to grieve for that lost magic, for the parents who had given her that brief, idyllic childhood.

Until she did, and came to terms with their deaths, she would never be completely healed.

Healed? That was a strange word to use. But here, in the peace of the lake, she knew that there was something wrong with her, something that did need healing. And perhaps this was where she would find it, and know what her life ought to be.

Laurie shook herself impatiently and walked down the front steps of the porch, taking the little path that wound down through the grove of paper-birch trees to the little bay. She knew what her life was going to be, didn't she? Marriage to Alec. Keeping her career on for a while, then giving it up to raise their children, to be his wife and helpmeet. It was all planned.

But as she stood on the small beach, looking out past the rocky little headlands that enclosed the cove, it all seemed somehow far away. And those long-lost days, spent here with Russ and the others, seemed very close.

'Laurie!' Alec's voice sounded loud and impatient, jerking her out of her dream. 'Laurie, where——? Oh, there you are. What on earth are you doing down there? I thought we came to see the cottage.'

'This is all part of it.' Laurie waited for him to join her at the water's edge. 'Look—all this little bay is ours. We used to swim here—and Daddy used to swim far out into the lake and frighten us; we'd lose sight of him completely. If you paddle into the water a little way you can see the fishes' nests. They make them of stones—circles around a small depression in the bed of the lake.' She laughed at Alec's disbelieving face. 'They really do! Take off your shoes and socks and paddle out to see. They're not far out.'

'No, thank you.' He looked around. 'But it's quite attractive, I'll agree with you there. Is that jetty ours too?'

Laurie looked at him, a little startled. When she had used the word 'ours', she had been referring to her parents and herself, rather than Alec. But of course, when they were married...

'Yes,' she said. 'And that must be Uncle Tom's boat.'

They walked along the beach and along the tiny path that led to the jetty, at the end of one of the arms of the bay. The boat was moored firmly to a post. It was a small motor-boat, quite old but in good condition. Tom had always looked after his craft, she remembered.

'There ought to be canoes too. He liked paddling about quietly, watching the birds and animals. I suppose they're under the cottage.'

'I did see something there.' Alec was staring thoughtfully about him. 'You know, this could really be made very pleasant. And there's a lot of land about here that doesn't seem to be used. We could buy it— build some more cottages. Timeshare letting—that's the thing these days. This place has potential, Laurie, you realise that.'

'"Potential"...?' She looked at him, then at the quiet shore, thickly wooded. 'But I don't want——'

Alec laughed. 'You don't want anything to change, do you?' he said fondly. 'You just want it all to stay as it was when you were a child. Well, we all feel that, don't we? Nostalgia for the good old days. But you can't stand still, Laurie. Nothing stands still. If we don't do it, someone else will.' He took her arm. 'Let's go and look at the cottage, shall we?'

They walked back through the little grove and up the steps to the double doors. Laurie unlocked them and fastened them back, letting the mesh screen-doors swing shut behind her as she stepped into the big main room of the cottage. She stood in the dimness, her heart racing a little.

'Well, it's quite a good size,' Alec commented. 'Just the one room, is there?'

'One living-room, yes.' She looked around. It was so much as she remembered it; yet she had barely given it a thought for years. She felt almost as if she had just run in, an eight-year-old child, wet from swimming.

The kitchen end of the room was just as her mother had had it, with the big table by the window where they had eaten their meals, a huge refrigerator that must have been brought in by Uncle Tom, but the same benches and sink and—could it be?—the same cooker. At the other end was the big fireplace, where roaring log fires had been lit on winter evenings when they had only been able to reach the cottage on skis, the sofas and armchairs, looking even more battered than they did in her memory, the bookshelves and lamps, the rug her mother had made herself.

So little had changed since she had last been here; yet so much.

Alec nodded towards the six steps which rose from the middle of the room, opposite the door. 'Bedrooms?'

'Yes. Two.' Laurie led the way up the steps. 'This was my parents' room.' It was a nice room, too—large and airy, with a warm, cosy feeling. The big bed was covered by the patchwork quilt she remembered her mother sewing; it had taken her two winters to com-

plete, and it had only been on the bed for three weeks
when—— Abruptly, Laurie turned and led the way
out to the second room. 'I used to sleep here,' she
said. 'And sometimes I'd bring a friend with me. We
used to giggle all night long, it seemed.'

Next to the small bedroom was the bathroom, tiny
but neat with the tiles her father had put up. There
was no bath, only a shower, but who needed a bath,
Laurie's parents asked, when there was a whole lake
on the doorstep?

'And that's it,' she concluded, leading the way down
the steps again. 'Not luxury, I know—but all you need
for a lake cottage.'

'Hmm. Perhaps.' Alec stood in the middle of the
room, looking around assessingly. 'One could do a
lot with it, though. Make quite a few improvements.
As I said, Laurie, it has potential.'

'"Potential"?' she repeated, as she had done
earlier. 'But what sort of "potential", Alec?
Timeshare—filling the lakeside with cottages, selling
them by the week to people who just want to come
to enjoy the pleasures they can have any day in the
city? With a leisure centre, where they can swim in a
man-made pool, sit in a jacuzzi, use a gym instead of
going outside for their exercise? With a sophisticated
bar, a dance-floor, maybe a nightclub? Is that what
you've got in mind?'

'That's it exactly!' Alec cried, mistaking her horror
for enthusiasm. 'I knew you'd see it as soon as we
got here. Laurie, you've put into words exactly what
I had in mind—oh, yes, I knew we'd think alike on
this. We'll get moving on it straight away—get that
ridiculous condition overturned, and find someone to
draw up some plans. And then we'll——'

'Over my dead body!' a voice interrupted, and they both whirled to see a tall, dark shape silhouetted in the doorway. Laurie gasped, her hand going automatically to her throat, and Alec took a step forward. But, before he could speak, the figure disengaged itself from the doorway and moved forwards. The shadow lifted from his face.

'Brandon!' Alec exclaimed. 'What in hell's name are you doing here?' And Laurie, feeling suddenly dizzy, sank into one of the armchairs and stared up at him. Russ gave her a brief glance.

'What am I doing here? I came to see who was in the cottage, of course. We tend to watch out for each other around the lake—if we think there might be something wrong, we investigate. Besides, as you know, Tom was a friend of mine.'

Laurie stared at him. 'You mean your cottage is near here?'

'Certainly. I thought I'd told you.' He waved a hand towards the lake. 'It's on one of the islands. But never mind that—what was it I heard you saying, just as I came in?'

Alec gave him a cold glance.

'I don't really know what business it is of yours, Brandon,' he said stiffly, 'but Laurie and I were just discussing the potential this place has. If I'm right in thinking there's nobody building on the land in the immediate vicinity, then there's scope for a big development here. Quite a lot of it goes with the cottage anyway. And I've been wanting to diversify for some time—computers are all very well, but it's foolish to have all one's eggs in the same basket. Laurie agrees with me that there's a great potential here.'

'Which will be exploited, as I said, over my dead body.' Russ's voice was grim. He glanced at Laurie again. 'Do you really want to do that? Ruin everything about the area? Turn the lake into nothing more than a glorified holiday camp?'

Laurie opened her mouth, but Alec spoke quickly and angrily.

'There's no question of ruining the area. What we have in mind would enhance it—the land's little more than a jungle at present. A few tastefully designed cabins—anyway, it's really nothing to do with you, Brandon. It's for Laurie to decide. It's her property.'

'Not,' Russ said silkily, 'until she fulfils the conditions of the will. Not until she's lived here for three months.'

There was a short silence. Then Alec laughed.

'We'll have that overturned in no time. You said yourself it wouldn't stand up.'

'It could. If someone opposed your application. If old Tom's lawyer fought for it to be upheld.'

Alec stared at him. He laughed again, but there was an uneasy note in his laughter. 'It wouldn't be worth your while.'

'It would,' Russ asserted, and this time there was iron in his voice, cold, hard iron. 'It would be well worth my while to prevent such vandalism taking place on this lake. Well worth my while to save it from marauders such as you.' His glance swept over them both, and Laurie, feeling the lash of it, cringed as if it were a whip. 'Just you try,' he said softly, 'just you try.'

He turned on his heel and left the cottage. Laurie started up from her chair and made to follow him. 'Russ——' But Alec caught at her arm and held her firmly.

'Let him go. He can't really interfere with us.' His eyes were glinting with something she recognised as excitement—the excitement of a challenge. 'And if he tries—well, he'll find it's not so easy to put a spoke in the wheel of Alec Hadlow. We'll build that time-share development here, Laurie, and if Russ Brandon doesn't like it—well, he can just go and jump in the lake!' And, laughing heartily at his joke, he turned and went out through the door.

Laurie stared after him. She felt sick and shaken. She had never seen that look in Alec's eyes before, never realised so sharply that money was his god. Nor had she ever realised quite how much he disliked being opposed. He had seen Russ's intervention as an invitation to battle. And he wouldn't be satisfied until he had won.

But Russ Brandon had looked equally implacable. As if he too had no intention of losing this fight. And his hard, lean strength had made Alec's city appearance seem not urbane and sophisticated, but soft and flabby.

Laurie shivered. How had she come to be here, caught between these two men, caught between two lives? And all because of a lakeside cottage that she hadn't visited for seventeen years?

It had taken considerable courage for Laurie to go to Russ's office when she and Alec returned from their disastrous visit to the lake. But she knew that there was no choice to be made—she had to go, had to tell him her decision. He was her uncle's lawyer, after all, and held the title to the property until it could be passed to her, or sold for charity.

She dressed carefully for the meeting. A slim skirt and jacket worn open over a light blouse, casual but smart, the understated elegance of the cut and the fabric all that were needed to display its quality. A slender gold chain round her neck, small gold earrings, and her fingers bare. The kind of dressing that set off her dramatic looks and brought heads turning in the most exclusive restaurants, yet which gave no room for doubt that here was a woman with both brains and ability.

Just let Russ Brandon try to put her down—just let him try!

This time, Russ did not come to meet Laurie at the lift. When she walked through the door of his office, he was standing at the huge window, staring out over the city. She stepped forwards, and he turned and gave her a sombre look.

'Laurie.'

'Russ,' she responded formally, and looked past him at the city that shimmered below them in the July heat. 'It's a beautiful day.'

He inclined his head, but did not reply. He moved to his desk and stood behind it for a moment, fingering the files which lay on it. He did not offer her coffee.

'Why don't you sit down, Laurie? We may as well discuss this in a civilised manner.' He lowered himself into his chair and looked at her again. Laurie felt uncomfortable.

'Why are you looking at me like that? What are you thinking?'

His eyes moved over her. They looked darker this morning, the blue of a sky heavy with thunder. There was no hint of a smile in their depths—but had she expected one?

'I'm wondering just how anyone can change so much,' he said at last. 'In so many ways, you could be the old Laurie, even though you were just a child when I saw you last. You have the same eyes—that strange green, like a cat looking out of the shadows. The same smile curves your mouth and makes me want to smile back. You even laugh in the same way. Yet—in every other way, you're a stranger. You're a paradox, Laurie. And I can't quite come to terms with it.'

Laurie's discomfort increased; she tried to feel indignant—didn't she have the right to feel indignant?—but it wouldn't come. Instead, to her dismay, she felt the prick of tears. She bit her lip, but held his gaze.

'I don't know what you're talking about, Russ. Of course I've changed—I've grown up. And I didn't come here to talk about myself.'

'You asked me what I was thinking,' he pointed out. 'And I can see you've grown up, Laurie. Nobody could miss the fact that you're a woman, and a very attractive one at that. That isn't the change I meant. Nor the fact that you look more at home now in smart city clothes than I think you would in the shorts and shirt you lived in as a little girl. Although that's the kind of change I mean—the change from a tomboy who loved the country and all it stood for, to a sophisticated city woman who wouldn't know a loon from a beaver any more.'

'I would!' This time she could feel indignant, and she had no scruples in letting her indignation show.

'That's ridiculous, Russ. I love the country just as much as ever. I love the lake——'

'And that's why you haven't been near it for seventeen years, I suppose,' he shot back at her. 'That's why you never even contacted your uncle, and left him to die alone——'

'No! No, that's not true!' Her denial was a cry of pain. 'I didn't even know Uncle Tom was ill.'

'You never enquired,' he said coldly. 'Not in seventeen years.'

'I was only eight——'

'You were eight for only a few months after you left Kingston,' Russ said bluntly. 'Then you were nine, then ten—and you've got as far as twenty-five without giving him a thought. You can't use the excuse of being only a child, Laurie. It might have meant something to begin with, but it hasn't now for the past ten years. You could have contacted Tom at any time. You could have visited him.'

Laurie was silent. She felt as if she had been whipped. There was nothing she could say in answer to Russ's accusations. They were true. There had been nothing to prevent her getting in touch with her uncle again, once she was old enough to decide for herself. Nothing.

Only the conditioning of John and Ella Marchant.

She looked at Russ, her green eyes shimmering with tears. How could she possibly explain to him what it had been like, living with the Marchants? How could she make him see the effect they had had on her when she had come to them, shocked, frightened, bewildered? How their home had been for so long the only place where she could be safe, where nothing dangerous ever happened? How she had accepted their ruling that a clean break with her previous life was the best thing for her?

'I didn't think Uncle Tom wanted me to contact him,' she said at last. 'Russ, when I left Kingston it was as if I came to another planet. I never heard from anyone there. Perhaps I would have gone back eventually, if only out of curiosity. But I never had any hint that anyone *wanted* me to go back.'

Russ opened his mouth to speak, then hesitated. As if he'd thought better of what he wanted to say, he turned aside and picked up the file that she recognised from her previous visit. He opened it and looked down at the papers it contained.

'Well, there's no sense in going over old ground again. You've come to see me about the cottage. And the condition old Tom laid on your inheriting it.'

'That's right. And I haven't much time—Alec's meeting me for lunch. So if we could get on with the business...'

'Certainly.' Russ's tone was formal. 'There isn't much to be said, after all. You know the condition—that you should live there for a minimum of three months. That's what Tom wanted.' Russ laid the papers down and sat back, watching her through narrowed eyes.

'But you did say that such a condition could probably be overturned,' Laurie said quietly.

'I did. I also said it could be fought.'

'And you would fight it?'

'I certainly would. Especially now that I know what your plans are for the place.'

Laurie stared at him. She had been startled by Alec's enthusiasm for the timeshare concept. But since their return to Ottawa they had talked, and, although he had not been able to convince her that he was right, they seemed to be working towards a compromise. A few cabins, dotted among the trees, he'd said— nothing large, nothing obtrusive, just a few places of a high standard that the firm could use. Give holidays to those who might otherwise not be able to have one, he'd said persuasively, families with children who would enjoy the lake... And Laurie, thinking of her own childhood, had agreed that this could be a good idea.

But why should she tell Russ Brandon this? Her plans—Alec's plans—were no business of his. He would probably oppose them anyway. He wanted the lake for himself; he'd oppose any new cottage being built, any new people coming to enjoy what he'd come to think of as his own.

'Any plans Alec and I make are our own private affair——' she began, but he interrupted.

'They're very much my affair too, and any right-thinking person's. Anyone concerned with the environment would be appalled to hear what you two were planning last weekend.'

Laurie wanted to tell him that they hadn't both been making the plans he had been so appalled by—they were Alec's, and against her own wishes. But loyalty to her fiancé forbade this. Instead, she took refuge in defensiveness.

'You'd have plenty of opportunity to object to our plans once they were made public,' she said. 'You might even find you approved of them——'

'Never!'

'—but, of course, you wouldn't give us the chance, would you? You'd rather fight from the start, without even knowing what you were fighting. You'd rather keep the lake for yourself than let anyone else near it, and that's the truth behind this—that you hate the idea of anyone else enjoying *your* lake. Isn't it?'

Russ's face darkened. 'I've no objection to other people enjoying any of the lakes, in the right way. But what you are suggesting—leisure centres, theme parks——'

'We never suggested a theme park!'

'Maybe not. But it would be next on your list.' He stood up, looming over her, and she felt suddenly frightened. 'I warn you, Laurie, that I shall fight you on this. And I'll start by insisting that Tom's condition be met. You can fight me if you like. But it will be a lengthy, time-wasting and expensive fight. Are you prepared for that, you and that smooth fiancé of yours?'

Laurie stared up at him. Then she too stood up. She placed her hands flat on his desk and leaned forwards, so that their faces were close. She was conscious of an odd feeling, somewhere low in her stomach, but she ignored it. She met his eyes, green clashing with dark, stormy blue.

'There will be no fight through the courts,' she told him quietly. 'I'll take my inheritance, and there will be nothing you can do to prevent me. I'll fulfil Uncle Tom's conditions. I'll go and live at the cottage for three months. And then—we shall see.'

There was a moment of complete silence. Laurie was very conscious of Russ Brandon's face, so close to hers. She could feel her heart hammering, almost hear the blood pulsing round her body.

'You'll never stand it,' Russ said at last, and Laurie, with a feeling of triumph, drew back and picked up her shoulder-bag.

'We'll see,' she said again, and looked down at the papers that lay on his desk. 'Now—is there anything I should sign before I leave? Or do I have to complete my three months' stay first?'

CHAPTER FOUR

SUNLIGHT slanted across the wooden floor, turning it to gold, as Laurie woke next morning. She lay for a moment looking through the screened window at the pattern of leaves dancing against the sky, feeling the fresh, cool breeze on her face.

With a sudden feeling of excitement, she slid out of bed and ran barefoot down the steps and across the living-room. Outside, the lake was alive, tiny waves sparkling against the dark green backdrop of the far shore. Laurie, wearing only the light cotton shirt she had slept in, slipped out through the door and down the narrow path to the shore. She stopped with her toes touching the cool water and, with a swift movement, unbuttoned the shirt, threw it to the grassy bank behind her, and ran into the water.

It was colder than she had expected, and she gasped as it struck against her warm skin. She ran on, feeling icy droplets flick against her shoulders and breasts, and then let herself fall forwards to swim out into the lake, beyond the bay. This was what her father had loved to do in the mornings, calling to his wife to come with him, and they had swum together, as close sometimes as if they were in an embrace, laughing and splashing each other with bright drops of water.

Laurie turned in the water and looked back at the shore. The cottage was almost hidden among its grove of trees, their slender white trunks bending gracefully in a fall of whispering leaves. There were no other cottages near by. The shore was wooded, with smooth rocks sloping down to the water.

She swam parallel with the shore for a while, then turned on her back and floated, gazing idly up at the sky. The initial coolness of the water had disappeared, and she was warm, feeling the sun on her bare skin. Dazzled by the brightness, she closed her eyes.

'Well, well, well. The mermaid of the lake. But I'm afraid you won't lure many sailors to their doom around here.'

The voice broke upon the stillness as if it had come out of the air, and Laurie's eyes flew open. She moved sharply in the water, choking a little as a wave splashed over her face, and looked up to see Russ Brandon grinning at her from a canoe. Aware of her nakedness, she felt her face flame.

'What on earth do you think you're playing at?' she demanded, treading water. 'Creeping up on me like that—you nearly frightened me out of my skin!'

'And that would have been a pity,' he drawled, 'your skin being so very attractive—from what I've seen of it.' He must have seen plenty of it, she thought with a fresh wave of colour scorching her cheeks. How long had he been watching her as she floated on her back, her eyes closed? 'But you shouldn't expose it to too much sunshine. It would be a shame to burn it, and it looks *very* delicate.'

'A gentleman wouldn't have been looking,' she retorted, and he laughed.

'Then I've never met a gentleman in my life. Come on, Laurie, you can't expect to disport yourself naked around a lake and not get stared at.'

'I didn't think there was anyone here to stare,' she said coldly. 'And I wish you'd stop doing it now.'

'Dare say you do,' he replied cheerfully, 'but then, I'm not a gentleman, am I? I'm just the boy next door, remember? And it's not the first time I've seen you in the buff. I was in and out of your house every day at one time.'

'That was when I was a child—before I——' she floundered, and he laughed again.

'Before you grew up into a very beautiful woman and acquired your layer of sophistication. And kept a modesty that I find quite surprising. I thought you feminists weren't bothered about that kind of thing.'

'Did I ever say I was a feminist?'

'Well, aren't you? You have a career, you do your own thing.'

'That's just being a person.' This was a ridiculous conversation to be having out here in the lake, with herself treading water and Russ's eyes gleaming as he looked down at her from his perch in the canoe. Why couldn't he go away? But he showed no signs of wanting to move.

'Of course, you're embarking on an old-fashioned marriage, aren't you?' he said thoughtfully. 'Company wife and all that. Society hostess. No, I suppose there's not much feminism about that.' He looked down at her and lifted one eyebrow. 'And what does Mr Hadlow think of his future wife behaving like a mermaid in the lake, hmm? Or doesn't he know? Doesn't he swim?'

Laurie realised that Russ thought Alec was here with her at the lake. He thought they were still engaged. She opened her mouth to tell him that the engagement was off, then hesitated. Somehow, unable to hide her body from his interested gaze, she thought it might be a good idea if he didn't know that she had offered Alec his ring. But she couldn't pretend he was with her—it would be too easy for Russ to find out the truth.

'Alec's not here,' she admitted reluctantly. 'He had to go back to Toronto.'

'So you're here by yourself? For the whole three months?'

'Unless he comes to join me,' she said, knowing that he wouldn't.

'Well, imagine that. Aren't you going to be lonely?'

'Didn't you think of that when you insisted I should come?' she asked sharply. 'I suppose it never occurred to you that it might not be convenient. Alec couldn't take three months off to lounge about here—and it wasn't easy for me, either. But that would never have struck you, would it?'

'I didn't make the condition,' he said mildly. 'It was Tom's idea, not mine. And I think he considered it was important for you, whether it was difficult or convenient or not. Maybe more important than keeping your high-flying job. After all, you could always have refused. Several charities would have benefited if you had.'

Laurie was silent. She looked around her at the glittering lake, the blue sky. A loon flew low, skimming the surface, its dark wings beating slowly. It settled on the water and she could see the black and white stripes on its neck. She remembered the cry she had heard the night before, the wild lament echoing across the lake, something Alec had probably never heard. It had seemed to call to her, to plead with her. Had her uncle known that she needed to be here, to hear that cry, to understand what it was asking?

'You'll get cold,' Russ said, his voice suddenly gentle. 'Do you want me to take you back?'

Laurie looked up at him again, drawing in her breath sharply as she thought of climbing into his canoe, naked, having to feel his hands on her body as he helped her, having to sit there, totally exposed to his gaze. 'No—thank you!'

He smiled. 'Then you'd better start swimming. We could chat much more comfortably than this over a cup of coffee, don't you think?'

'Perhaps—if we had anything to chat about,' she retorted, and turned in the water to swim away from him. And knew that as she let her body float to the surface, as she moved her legs and arms in the slow, gentle stroke that would take her back to the little cove, he must be watching her still, watching her movements, letting his eyes move over her bare limbs, her back, the smooth roundness of her hips.

There was nothing to be done about it. But she would not risk it happening again. From now on she would be clad in a swimsuit, the least revealing one she possessed, every time she came anywhere near the water. Laurie swam steadily away. Then she turned and glanced back, expecting to see Russ still looking after her. But he had gone.

For a moment she stared, unable to believe that he could have disappeared. And then she saw his canoe already heading for the far side of the lake, little more than a patch of colour against the darkness of the shore. He must have started to paddle as soon as she'd begun to swim. Laurie swam slowly on and waded from the water, picking up her shirt as she went.

She had an odd, wholly unreasonable feeling of disappointment.

*　　*　　*

Laurie saw no more of Russ for a few days. She un-packed her car, stacking away the food she had brought with her and sorting out her clothes. When planning her stay, she had looked through her wardrobe and realised that few of her existing outfits were suitable for cottage life. Elegant suits and dresses were scarcely likely to be needed, and she possessed few of the casual trousers and shorts that would be comfortable to wear. She had bought several pairs, together with some new shirts and sweaters; warm though it was now, she expected to be here until the autumn, and there were bound to be cooler days and evenings.

The cottage too needed some attention. Uncle Tom had been a casual housekeeper, and Laurie spent some time shifting everything outside in order to have a thorough clean. Luckily, her parents had built it for easy maintenance, and it needed little more than a thorough sweeping and dusting, with a good deal of accumulated rubbish to be stowed away in the big space below the building, for later disposal. She had almost finished, and was struggling to move the sofa back through the open doors, when a shadow fell across her and she looked up, knowing who it must be.

'Quite the little housewife,' Russ Brandon said, smiling, and Laurie, already hot, sticky and irritated, brushed her hair away from her eyes and snapped at him.

'Hadn't you better make up your mind just what I am? A mermaid—a housewife—I seem to fulfil all roles in your mind. Or maybe you just like to stereotype people?'

He stared at her for a moment, his eyes travelling down her dusty figure. 'You've got a smear of grease on your nose,' he remarked. 'And isn't it rather a shame to wear your best clothes for work like this? We don't generally dress up to do our chores around here—or were you expecting someone to drop in?'

Exasperated, Laurie turned back to the sofa.

'I really don't see what business it is of yours what I wear—or don't wear.' She saw him grin, and belatedly recalled the fact that on their last meeting she had been wearing precisely nothing. Her face burned. 'Excuse me. I'm trying to get this back through the doors.'

'Here, let me give you a hand,' he said, but Laurie brushed him aside.

'Thank you, I can manage perfectly well myself. I got it out here, after all.'

Instantly, he stood back and watched while she strained to get the unwieldy piece of furniture through the doorway. How on earth had she managed to manoeuvre it out in the first place? Had its legs gone through first, had she had it on its side? She couldn't for the life of her remember—and it didn't help, having this aggravating man standing there watching. If only she hadn't been so quick to refuse his offer— but she wouldn't retract now and ask his help. No, she'd get it through somehow even if it took—all— night...

'Look, you can't manage it.' His voice was shaking with laughter. 'Let me do it. You'll hurt yourself.'

'I told you, I can manage,' Laurie said through her teeth, and this time when he spoke there was irritation in his voice.

'Don't be so childish! Honestly, Laurie, sometimes
you behave as if you're still eight years old. What is
it with you, arrested development, or are you just too
plain stubborn ever to admit you can't do something?
Does it *matter* if I give you a hand? Will the earth
fall in? Or are you afraid there'll be strings attached?'

Laurie stopped and stared at him. 'Strings? I don't
know what you mean.'

Russ looked at her. His eyes held hers for a breath-
taking second, then moved slowly, lazily, down her
body. His glance lingered on her breasts, slid down
to her waist, her brief shorts, her suntanned legs. He
moved forward, almost casually, and laid his hands
on her waist. She felt his fingers splayed across her
body, and caught her breath. 'Russ——'

Russ bent his head and touched her lips with his.
For the tiniest part of a second, Laurie wanted to
recoil. But, at the movement of her head, one hand
moved swiftly up to keep her firmly in position, and
then his mouth was moving on hers, shaping her lips
to his kiss, and she no longer had the power to resist.
She felt his tongue touch the softness of her mouth,
probing gently, as light as the brush of a butterfly's
wings, and her lips parted to allow its exploration.
His hand tightened behind her head, and she felt him
move, touching her breast with his other hand, his
fingertips on her trembling skin. Without thought,
without planning, she slid her hands around his neck
and held him to her, knowing that if he let her go she
would fall.

Russ brought the kiss to an end, leaving her lips
with the softness with which he had begun, and put
her gently away from him. Laurie opened her eyes

and stared up at him, shaken and quivering. His eyes were dark.

'Those sort of strings,' he said, a husky note in his voice, and turned away. He took a firm grip on the legs of the sofa. 'I mean, I'm not going to want payment for helping you with this,' he went on, lifting it towards him. 'I'm not going to ask that we test it out together once we get it into place. I'm not,' he enunciated carefully, 'going to expect you to sleep with me.'

Laurie gasped. She grabbed at the other two legs and tried to wrench it away from him. The memory of the kiss, only just behind her, was already scorching her with embarrassment, with shame. How could she have let him do that? How could she have even begun to respond?

'I never dreamed of even thinking you might be! It would never have occurred to me to think such a thing. And, even if you were, there would be no chance, believe me. I wouldn't sleep with you if you were the last man on earth, you know that? So the question of—of doing it just because you helped me move my furniture——'

'Doesn't arise either,' he said grimly, not letting go. 'That was precisely what I was trying to make clear. Laurie, for heaven's sake, stop struggling with this thing and co-operate. Look, if we lift it a bit and you swing your end round there, I can get these legs past the doorway. Then—that's it—all we need to do is work it forwards a bit, and then you twist it back a bit—carefully, or you'll have a leg through the glass—— Now, we're nearly there; just ease it round a bit more and—presto! It's in. See? It only wanted a bit of co-operation. Like so many other things in life.'

Laurie set down her end, and stood panting slightly. The kiss was still burning in her mind. She looked at the sofa, standing in the middle of the floor almost grinning at them, and then looked up at Russ. He was watching her, a half-mocking smile tugging at his lips. Reluctantly, ruefully, she smiled back.

'I suppose I'd better say thank you. I'd never have got it in on my own. Would you like a drink?'

'Not the most gracious thanks I've ever received, but more than I've come to expect of you,' he remarked, shifting the sofa across the floor. 'Where do you want this? Where Tom used to have it? And yes, please, I would like a drink. Something long and cold.'

Laurie went to the refrigerator and took out two cans. She opened them and poured the drink into the glasses, added ice, and then hesitated. 'Shall we take it out to the porch?'

'That would be pleasant,' he said gravely, and they went out to sit in the old chairs that Laurie had found in the cellar and brought out. There was a table too, made from an old barrel cut in half, and she set the glasses down on it.

'I see you've got the hummingbird-feeder up,' Russ remarked after a moment or two. 'What have you got in it? Sugar-water?'

Laurie nodded. 'I remember my mother doing it. The birds have found it already—ruby-throats, aren't they? There's one now.' They watched as the tiny bird, brilliant as a jewel, hovered by the feeder, its long, thin bill sucking out the sweet mixture. Its minute wings moved so fast that they were no more than a blur of colour. After a few seconds it shot away with a 'whoomph' of soft sound. 'They're beautiful,' Laurie said softly.

Russ was watching her curiously. She turned her head, aware of his eyes on her, and caught a softness in his expression, gone almost before she recognised it. She felt a quick leap of her heart and looked away again quickly. The silence stretched between them and she could think of nothing to say to break it.

'How much do you remember of those days?' Russ asked after a moment. 'Has it all disappeared? You were very young.'

'I remember quite a lot,' she said slowly. 'Especially about being here. You used to come with your brothers and camp on the grass.' They both looked towards the space at the side of the cottage, where Russ and his two brothers had erected their tent. 'I could look out of my window and see you there in the mornings.'

He nodded. 'We'd get up early and go fishing some mornings—but, however quiet we were, we never managed to get away without you waking up and creeping out to beg to come with us.'

'Did you try?' Laurie asked, thinking what a nuisance she must have been to the teenage brothers.

'Not really. You were fun—a good kid, always ready to try anything, always ready to take a joke. We never minded you tagging along.' He grinned. 'Anyway, you were part of the package. You came with the cottage. We couldn't really drown you, tempted though we might have been at times.'

Laurie laughed. 'I remember those times very well. I caught quite a few fish of my own. We'd come back and barbecue them for breakfast. It was fun.'

Russ looked at her. 'It could be fun again, Laurie. There's no reason on earth why we shouldn't do those things now.'

Laurie met his eyes. There was a curious darkness in them, a depth she had never before encountered. She felt a shiver touch her spine.

'No,' she said quickly, feeling like a snail withdrawing the stalks of its eyes because they had been touched, however lightly. 'No, I don't think so, Russ. Thanks all the same.'

There was a slight pause. She stared at her glass, feeling uncomfortably warm. She had been rude—but there was something about Russ that made her want to back off. Something that—well, almost scared her.

'Fiancé wouldn't like it?' Russ said lightly, and she opened her mouth to tell him that she had no fiancé now, then closed it again. She'd already decided it was better if he thought the engagement was still on. Now, feeling the strange electricity that crackled between them, she was certain she was right.

'If you like,' she replied, her voice brittle. She picked up her glass and drained it. 'Now, if you don't mind, I've got a lot to do. I want to finish this cleaning today and——'

'Why? Lord and master coming for the weekend?'

'No,' she said quietly. 'I just want to get it done.'

Russ stretched himself luxuriously in his chair.

'That's what I love about cottage life,' he remarked as if to the trees. 'There's never any hurry. Never any pressure. It's so different from city life—wouldn't you agree?'

'I'll give it some thought when I've finished this job,' Laurie told him, and Russ laughed and swung himself to his feet.

'Laurie, you slay me,' he declared, 'you really do!' And, before she could protest, he had caught her face between both his hands, lifted her slightly to meet his bent head, and kissed her gently on the lips.

'I'll be around,' he said, vaulting over the balustrade of the porch and dropping lightly to the ground. 'Maybe next time you won't be quite so busy. Or maybe you'll be dressed for some other chore that must be done—lumberjacking, or damming the lake. Only we do have beavers to do that sort of work for us, you know.'

It seemed very quiet when he had gone. And the feel of his lips on hers, firm yet sweet, lingered for a long while. Laurie found herself touching her mouth gently, several times, as if to assure herself that it had really happened. But why should she want it to be true? Wouldn't it be much better if it had *not* happened?

Russ Brandon! she thought crossly as she shifted the rest of the furniture back and arranged Uncle Tom's books on the shelves. Why couldn't he just keep away?

But it seemed that Russ either couldn't or didn't want to keep away. Almost every day, Laurie would catch a glimpse of him drifting by in his sailing dinghy, or skimming across the bay on his sailboard with its brilliant sail like a bird's wing on the shimmering water, or flashing past with a burst of foam in his small, fast motor-boat. Or maybe, at dusk, she would see his canoe, a silhouette against the burning sunset, paddle silently past as he went beaver-watching along the shores. And she would remember when she had gone too, a small girl tagging along with the older boys, willing to do whatever they required of her just so that she could be part of their lives.

Russ seemed intent on convincing her that she was no longer a part of his life. So why didn't he just stay away? Why did he have to keep reminding her that he was around?

Irritated and tantalised, Laurie made up her mind that she wouldn't even notice him—at least, that she wouldn't let him see that she'd noticed him. She went about her business as if she were blind to his comings and goings, never glancing up as he tacked into the bay with his dinghy, looking the other way when his sailboard came into sight, busy with some task when his motor-boat shot past. But she couldn't pretend to ignore him when he paddled into the bay one evening and invited her to go and hunt beavers with him.

'Come on,' he urged as she hesitated on the beach, wondering how he had managed to creep up on her so silently. She hadn't even known he was there until he'd spoken, and then, to her annoyance, she'd almost toppled off the jetty into the water. 'You used to love it when you were a kid, remember? But I suppose you're too sophisticated now for such simple pleasures. After all, you can see beavers any day in a zoo.'

That stung her. 'I don't go to zoos,' she retorted shortly. 'I don't like seeing caged animals.'

'Then come and see some in their natural habitat,' he said, and, unable to think of any reason why not, she climbed into the canoe and silently fastened the life-jacket he handed her.

They paddled out of the bay, Russ in the stern and Laurie in the bow. The sun was low, turning the sky to a golden dome arching above them, and the lake lay ahead like a sheet of hammered copper. The trees along the far shore were starkly black against the burning sky. There was no sound but the soft whisper of their paddles, and then the sudden wild call of the loon—a lament that echoed with bitter sadness across the lake. Laurie paused, feeling its sorrow pulse through her body. It seemed at that moment to express all the longing she felt on evenings like this, the yearning for something she had never had, yet could never describe.

'It's an evocative sound, isn't it?' Russ said quietly from behind her, and she nodded, unable to speak.

'I used to hear it in dreams,' she revealed, speaking as if to herself. 'After I'd left here—after... I never knew quite what it was—that sound. It was as if I'd blocked it out, that and the other memories. But when I heard it again, the first night I was back here, I remembered at once. And I knew what my dreams had been about and why I used to wake from them feeling so sad, so lost.'

The man behind her said nothing. She dipped her paddle into the water, feeling again that yearning that had followed her through her childhood. The sense that something precious had gone from her life—been stolen from her. Yet who had stolen it? Just what had happened out here all those years ago?

She wondered suddenly if she'd been wise to come back. Wasn't it better to do as her aunt and uncle had always believed, and shut that part of her life away, pretend it had never happened? Weren't some things better left buried, forgotten? Especially when you were adult, and had control of your life, when you knew who you were and where you were going...

But did she know those things? Was she really sure?

They paddled on. Sometimes, on evenings like this, you could see beavers swimming close to the lodges they had built from fallen trees and branches.

Sometimes you could see them on land, rushing down the bank to throw themselves into the lake like children on their first sight of the water. You could hear the smack of their tails as they dived, see their round heads break the surface to peer about them.

But there were no beavers tonight. And soon, as dusk fell, the mosquitoes would emerge and find human flesh a feast. Russ turned the canoe and they began to paddle back.

'No luck tonight, I'm afraid,' he said, his voice little more than a murmur on the evening air. 'We'll try again some time, perhaps.'

Laurie nodded. The evening had darkened, the sky was now a deep azure with only a few coppery streaks to remind them of the sunset. The water rippled slow and heavy under the canoe and, when they reached the little bay and she stepped out, it was like cool silk around her ankles. She waded up on to the beach, and turned to say goodnight, but Russ had driven the canoe half out of the water and was getting out himself.

They walked up to the cottage, still not speaking. Laurie pushed open the screen-door and Russ followed her inside. She turned on the lamp, feeling him close behind her. Her heart was thudding in her breast, as if she had just run a race. Breathlessly, shaking a little, she ran her hands down over her hips, as if to assure herself that she was adequately clothed. The shorts she wore suddenly felt brief.

Russ laid his hands on her shoulders, and she felt the warmth of them like fire on her skin. He turned her slowly towards him. The lamplight glowed on his lean face and the light of fireflies danced in his eyes.

'Laurie . . . I've been thinking a lot about you. Ever since the other day, when we did our furniture-shifting . . .' A flicker of a smile touched his lips. 'I tried to keep away, to tell myself you weren't for me, we'd drifted too far apart, we're different people now. But seeing you here, day after day—messing about on the beach, paddling that old canoe of yours, the one Tom used to use, swimming so *respectably* clad now——' there was a laugh in his voice, but he was serious again as he continued '—it's brought it all back again. Laurie, you belong here. Can't you see that? You don't fit in with the city, with Toronto, with that smart-aleck fiancé of yours.' He smiled at the pun. '*This* is your place—just as it's mine.' He was drawing her close as he spoke, close against his body so that she could feel the hardness of his muscles, the lean strength of him from shoulder to thigh. 'Laurie . . .'

Laurie swayed against him. Her mind was whirling, the blood singing through her veins, burning into her head. She could not think, could only give herself up to the sensations he was waking in her body. The scorching touch of his fingers on her shoulders, her back . . . the shivering tingle as he ran a hand lightly down her spine, the shock as he touched her thigh below the hem of her shorts. And, when she looked up at him, her lips parted in a gasp, the feeling of drowning as he bent his head and laid his mouth upon hers.

His lips were firm, yet gentle. They shaped hers and held them as his tongue flicked into her open mouth, then darted away again. Laurie caught her breath. She was clinging to him now, without any knowledge of how her arms had come to be around him, and her hands were moving in his thick hair. She heard a tiny whimper and realised that it must have come from her own throat, for there was a deep growling sound emanating from Russ's chest. She pressed closer against him, bewildered by what was happening, yet wanting it too badly to think about the implications. The tingle that had started in her spine, in her stomach—she no longer knew where it had begun— was spreading over her whole body.

Russ lifted her and carried her to the old settee. He laid her down and knelt beside her. His lips moved over her face, exploring it as a blind person might explore with fingertips. One arm lay under her shoulders, the hand keeping her face turned towards him; the other hand circled her breasts, then slid down to caress her waist, her stomach, her soft, quivering thighs.

'Russ...'

'It's all right, my love,' he murmured against her throat, and she was silenced by his words. Again, her hands were in his hair, the fingers tangling in the thick locks, and as he kissed her again she felt his fingers at her breast, unfastening the buttons on her shirt. A moment later he was parting the thin fabric, his hand covering the fullness of her naked breast, and then he moved to press his lips against the swelling softness.

Laurie lay quite still. Alec had never kissed her in this way, never made such tender, delicate love to her. He had never touched her skin with this sure, gentle touch, never brought such a pulsating fire to her blood, never caused her body to tremble in his arms. Nor had any other man, for Laurie's experience of love was small. She had always drawn back, never wanted anyone—even the man she had promised to marry—to go this far.

How could she ever have believed herself in love with Alec?

She twisted suddenly in Russ's arms, wanting him to kiss her again, wanting his love with an urgency that was almost frightening. But, as if her thoughts had transmitted themselves to him, he drew suddenly away and pulled the edges of her shirt together over her breasts. She stared up at him and saw his face close, as if he had deliberately shut out all emotion.

'I'm sorry,' he said raggedly. 'I forgot. You aren't free to do this, Laurie. You've got a fiancé—or had you forgotten too?' To her dismay, there was an edge of contempt in his voice.

'No,' she insisted, struggling to sit up, reaching out her arms for him. 'No, Russ, it isn't——'

'Isn't important? Is that what you were going to say?' His voice was bitter as he rose to his feet. 'Just a bit of fun, a dalliance to while away the loneliness? Well, it's my own fault; I knew I shouldn't come, I knew I ought to leave you alone. But seeing you here— remembering . . .' His voice shook a little, and he stopped. She watched him, sensed the tension in him, realised that he was gathering himself together. 'I'll go now,' he said flatly. 'And rest assured, Laurie, I shan't be bothering you again. It's too dangerous.' He was looming over her now, staring down, his face shadowed, and when he spoke again his voice was soft, almost menacing. 'You're trouble, you know that? I saw it that first night, at your aunt's house. But, like a fool, I thought I could handle your sort of trouble. I find I can't—so I'll keep out of your way.'

He turned and strode across the room, and before Laurie, shocked and dismayed, could find words to stop him, he was gone, letting the mesh door swing closed behind him. And by the time she reached the steps his canoe had gone from the beach, and it was too dark now to see him out on the lake.

He would be chewed to bits by mosquitoes, Laurie thought irrelevantly as she went slowly back inside. And she wondered why, once again, she hadn't told him that her engagement to Alec was over.

Was it because she had been afraid of just what might happen if she did? Was she using Alec as a shield—a protection?

A protection against what?

CHAPTER FIVE

OVER the next few days Laurie worked harder than ever, though whether she was trying harder to clean the cottage or to push Russell Brandon from her mind she didn't know. But at last she finished her labours in the cottage, and felt pleased. The main room was light and airy, the big fan circling slowly in the middle of the ceiling; the sofa and chairs were old, their covers faded, but they had a comfortable look about them. The whole place, in fact, seemed to exude a subtle, welcoming tranquillity.

No wonder her uncle had spent his last years here, never wanting to leave. No wonder he had preferred to die here rather than in some old people's home in the city.

And he had wanted her to experience this peace too. He had felt, even though he had not seen her for so long, that she needed it. Indeed perhaps it was because he had not seen her for so long that he had *known* she needed it. Perhaps he was aware of what the city could do to a person.

Laurie went out on to the porch and looked down at the little crescent of beach. The tall grey figure of a heron was there, stalking delicately along the fringe of the water. Laurie watched as it lifted one foot, raised it high, then planted it with infinite care on the sand. She watched its slightly jerky movements as it poked its long neck forward, then the sudden stab of its long bill as it struck at a frog or small fish.

Apart from the heron, there was no living thing in sight. No loon skimmed across the glittering surface of the lake, no osprey soared high above it. Even the hummingbird-feeder hung neglected. It was almost as if the world had stopped breathing, as if Laurie and the heron were the only beings left.

Laurie sat down quietly on the top step of the porch. She watched the tall grey bird stalking along on its thin legs, poking its head forward with each step, and felt an almost superstitious link with it. While the heron was there, nothing could go wrong. While there were only the two of them, everything must be all right. She stared at it, willing it to stay, dimly aware of some unexplained fear that everything was about to be spoiled.

The heron stopped moving. It gathered its body into the hunched shape of an old man in a macintosh, sinking its long bill deep into its chest. There was a moment's breathless silence.

Then the sound of a car's engine broke upon the peace. It snarled its way down the track, and the heron unfolded its wings and lifted itself from the beach. Legs trailing, it flapped up and away, over the water and past the headland. And Laurie turned, with a sinking heart, knowing that her peace was about to be shattered like a fragile glass. She watched, not moving, as Alec's car bumped slowly down the last slope and turned in by the birch grove.

The door opened and Alec got out. Dressed in a city suit, his one concession to the heat being an open-necked shirt, he looked out of place among the trees. He walked across the grass, and Laurie waited, still not moving.

'So there you are.' He looked down at her, his eyes taking in her dusty shirt and shorts. 'You look like a charwoman,' he said disapprovingly.

'Probably because I've been working like one.' Laurie returned his look. 'Would you like a drink, Alec? It's a hot day.'

'It certainly is. Perhaps we could go inside—though I don't suppose it's any better, since you don't have air-conditioning.'

'Oh, the fan keeps things cool.' Laurie rose and led the way indoors. She went to the refrigerator and made two long iced drinks. 'Make yourself comfortable, Alec.'

He chose one of the armchairs and sat down, still looking out of place in the simple surroundings. Laurie sat opposite him, saying nothing. Presumably he would tell her soon why he had come.

'So how are you getting along here, Laurie? Finding it lonely?'

'No. It's so peaceful, so quiet.' She looked at him, wondering if he could possibly understand. 'It's . . . healing.'

'*Healing?* But you haven't been ill.'

'Not ill, no. But not really well, either.' She looked at him, her green eyes shadowed and thoughtful. 'I feel I've been—well, starved in a way, of something important, something I need. And here I've been finding it. It's doing me good, Alec. I need whatever's here—the peace, the quietness, the feeling that this is where life really matters, this is where the important things happen. Not in the cities, where everyone's lost sight of reality, but out here, close to the heart——' She stopped. Alec was staring at her, baffled. She knew that he had not understood a word.

'Laurie, you're mad!' he declared at last. 'This place has got to your mind; it's eating away at your brain. *This* is where important things happen? But *nothing* happens here. It's as quiet as the grave. And cities *are* reality. That's where life really goes on, where everything important is decided and implemented. All right, so you may be tired—you haven't had a real holiday in years, you've been working too hard, perhaps, and need a rest—but don't let it take you over, Laurie. Don't let it ruin your life—*our* life.'

' "Our life", Alec?' Laurie asked quietly.

'Yes, our life! Look, you didn't really expect me to believe you wanted to break our engagement, did you? You wouldn't have kept the ring otherwise. You knew I'd come back. Well, if it pleases you, I have. And I'm prepared to forget all that foolishness—let bygones be bygones.' He reached forward and took her hand before she could move it away. 'Let's stop being silly, Laurie, and go back to where we were. I've missed you.'

Looking at him, Laurie felt a pang of sorrow that she couldn't do as he wanted and tell him that she would, after all, become his wife. That simple statement might have won her back—but she knew now that she had never really loved Alec. She had seen him as a safe haven, a shelter from the real world. Now, after living alone by the lake, she had begun slowly to come to terms with her fears. She hadn't faced or overcome them all yet, but she was beginning to see that unless she did so she would never be a whole person.

She got up and went up the steps to her bedroom, returning with the box which contained her engagement-ring. Silently, she handed it to Alec, and he stared at it, then opened it and lifted out the glittering jewel.

'Take it back, Alec,' Laurie told him quietly, sitting down opposite him. 'It was never right for me anyway.'

He looked at her. Then he shook his head and reached across, taking her hand in his. 'Laurie, you don't mean this. It's just a whim—this place has got to your brain. You'll see; after a few weeks you'll be glad to come back to Toronto—glad to come back to me.' Before she could protest, he had slid the ring on to her finger again. 'How can you say it's not right for you? It's beautiful—exactly the kind of ring my wife ought to wear and be proud of. As I'm proud of you.'

Laurie felt a lump in her throat. How could she persuade him without hurting him? She shook her head.

'I'm sorry, Alec,' she said gently. 'It's not possible. I did mean it, you see, and—— Who's that?'

The sound of footsteps on the porch made her turn quickly. A stranger was approaching the door. She looked quickly at Alec, but he was already on his feet, an expansive smile on his face as he moved to welcome the newcomer.

'Ah, Morrison, there you are. Come in. Darling, this is Sam Morrison, a development architect. I was telling him about the cottage, and he offered to come out and have a look at it. Sam, this is my fiancée, Laurie Clive.' He smiled deprecatingly. 'She's been having a wonderful time playing housewife out here— finds it a relaxation from her high-powered job.'

Sam Morrison offered Laurie his hand. Dazed, she took it. She had stood up with Alec, and the three of them were now in a little knot in the middle of the room. His hand was cold, even on this hot day, and his thin face was pale, as if he never went out in the sun. He gave her a smile that revealed uneven and not very white teeth.

'I'm sorry,' she said. 'I don't understand. Did Alec ask you to come here?'

'Well, I don't know that you'd say he *asked*, exactly,' Morrison admitted, grinning at Alec. 'He was just telling me about this place you've got, and it seemed a good idea to both of us. And, I must say, it's got possibilities. Once the road's been made up, of course—that track wouldn't be any good at all.'

Laurie took a deep breath. She looked at Alec, then back at Morrison. 'I think you'd better tell me exactly what you mean.'

'Why, you know what we mean. We discussed it before—you and I.' Alec smiled, that indulgent smile that she realised she hated. 'The development we planned. I know you're not keen on a big timeshare complex—but something more discreet, in keeping, you'd have no objection to that. A few really exclusive cabins, each with its own private jetty—boats provided, of course—and a centre where everyone could come together, a small leisure centre with a gym, a really good little pool——'

Laurie opened her mouth to protest. A 'really good little pool'—with one of the prettiest lakes in Ontario on the doorstep? A gymnasium, with woodland trails stretching away in all directions? A leisure complex—*here*?

But already the two men had forgotten her. Alec was showing Sam Morrison around, displaying this, explaining that, his hands waving expansively. They went up the steps into the bedroom, and Laurie stared after them. She felt as if someone had kicked her in the stomach. She felt dazed, breathless.

How dared Alec bring this man here, as if it were his own property, as if she were prepared to agree to anything he suggested? How dared he assume that their engagement was still on, that she would welcome his return? The enormity of it left her stunned, and for a few minutes she was incapable even of moving.

A slight sound at the door caught at the edge of her attention, and she turned her head. Russ Brandon stood there, his tall frame silhouetted against the bright light outside. He was regarding her gravely.

Laurie gazed at him. She saw his strength, felt the power that emanated from him. She wanted suddenly to go to him, to run to the safety of that tall, broad body. But before she could move she felt a kick of something very like fear. Because Russ Brandon did not represent safety. There would be no haven from reality with him. He stood for life, with all its perils— and Laurie still wasn't sure that she could face anything as real and frightening as that. She wanted suddenly to retreat, to back away.

But Russ wouldn't let her. He came forward, caught her wrists, and held her close to him. His eyes were dark and smoky as he looked down at her, and Laurie felt her heart kick again and begin to race. Heat surged through her body. She lifted her face towards his, felt her lips part; she barely knew what she was doing, feeling, but as he drew her closer to him, so that she stood within the circle of his arms, she knew that this was what she wanted—had always wanted.

'Laurie,' he muttered, and his breath touched her face like the shadow of a kiss. 'Laurie, ever since I left you here the other day——'

There was a sharp sound from inside one of the bedrooms, and Laurie heard Alec's loud laugh. Russ dropped her hands, and she stepped away. Her heart was thumping and her knees felt shaky.

Russ's glance touched her face. 'I see you have visitors.'

'Yes.' Laurie glanced up at the steps leading to the bedrooms. 'Alec's here.'

As she spoke, the two men came into view. Morrison had taken out a notebook and was busy jotting something down. He smiled briefly at Laurie, as if she were of little account, then glanced at Russ, who stood as if made of stone. There was a moment's silence.

'Oh, hi,' Alec said without enthusiasm. 'Brandon again—you seem to make a habit of calling in here.' He looked at Laurie as if he would have more to say about this later.

'Just when I feel like it,' Russ replied equably. 'Of course, Laurie's been pretty busy—I don't disturb her unless she needs a hand.' He glanced at Sam Morrison again, and his face darkened.

'This is a friend of mine, Sam Morrison,' Alec said reluctantly. 'You've probably heard of Morrison and Ash, the land developers?'

'I have indeed.' Russ's tone hardened, and he looked quickly at Laurie. 'So you do intend to develop here.'

Laurie began to speak, to deny it, but Alec's voice drowned hers. 'Well, let's say we're looking at possibilities. Nothing decided just yet—Morrison's only just arrived. What about your own place, Brandon? Would you care to have him look that over while he's here? I'm sure he'd be glad to, wouldn't you, Sam?'

'Sure; it'd be a pleasure.' The uneven teeth showed briefly. 'We'd probably need to make you an offer for it anyway, if we decide to go ahead here. We'd want the place to be entirely exclusive.'

'Is there any other way?' Russ asked pleasantly, and the two men stared at him. He gave a short, mirthless laugh. 'Well, I'm afraid you'll be disappointed. I'm not interested in selling.'

Morrison gave him an uneasy smile, then turned to Alec. 'Perhaps we could have a look outside. There's quite a lot of land, you say?'

They brushed past, and Laurie was left in the dim, cool room with Russ. She stared at the floor, unable to think of anything to say. After a very long pause Russ spoke to her.

'Well?'

'Well what?' she whispered foolishly, and he moved then, put one hand under her chin and forced her to look at him. She met his eyes, knowing that her own must be clouded.

'So it was all lies,' he said slowly. 'All that you told me the other day—about loving the peace, feeling at home here—that was all talk. You didn't mean a word of it.'

'I did! I meant it all! Russ, you must believe me— I didn't know Alec meant to bring this man here. I didn't even know Alec was coming. It was a complete surprise——'

Russ dropped his hand away from her. 'Oh, come off it, Laurie! Why bother to lie to me? You know that if you live here for the requisite three months this place is yours, whether I like it or not. Why pretend you don't know and approve of everything Hadlow's doing?'

'But I don't! I don't approve. I never have.'

He gave her one look and she flinched away from it, away from the contempt of that searing ice-blue glance. She shook her head speechlessly, searching in vain for words that might convince him. She had to convince him—he must believe her, he *must*...

She lifted her hands, holding them out towards him, palms uppermost. And as Russ glanced down at them she realised that she was still wearing Alec's ring—that it showed on the inner side of her finger, and that Russ could not fail to see it.

She drew her hands back swiftly, but she was too late. He grasped them in his own, turned them over, and stared at the huge, flashing diamond. He lifted his head. His eyes were cold and hard as steel. He looked at her as if she was the lowest form of life he had ever encountered. And then he turned away, as if he could bear the sight of her no longer.

'Russ...' she whispered pleadingly. But he had gone. She heard his footsteps on the porch. She heard voices outside—Alec's loud and confident, Morrison's ingratiating, Russ's clipped and hard. Then the voices stopped.

Laurie crept to the door. Alec and Morrison were at the far side of the birch grove, looking speculatively over the bay. And out on the water, already little more than a spot of bright colour against the shimmering blue, was Russ's canoe, moving fast as he paddled back to the island that was his stronghold.

She got rid of them at last. Alec had clearly intended to take her back to Ottawa with him, the engagement resumed, but Laurie refused to go and he was unwilling to argue, with Sam Morrison as an interested bystander. He laughed that indulgent laugh and glanced at Morrison, shrugging his shoulders. 'Women! Stubborn as mules, but we wouldn't have 'em any other way, would we? And she's enjoying playing house.'

The patronising tone made Laurie seethe, but she restrained herself from retorting as she would have liked to. What was the point of quarrelling any more? All that mattered was to get rid of him and his horrible friend. And when at last she watched the two cars drive slowly away up the bumpy, rutted track, she felt a wave of relief.

She went back to the cottage. The sun was beginning to cast its coppery glow over the water. Dusk was spreading its shadows between the trees. The birds were settling in the trees and the first fireflies were lighting their flickering lamps.

But the tranquillity had been disrupted, the peace shattered, and it would not easily return. And as Laurie stood on the porch, breathing the cool air, she heard again the wild, lonely cry of the loon. And felt it as a lament for something she had lost, something she had never really known she possessed.

There was no sign of Russ on the lake for the next few days. Irritated by her own weakness, Laurie could not help looking out for his canoe whenever she was near the water. Normally, she had caught a glimpse of him at least once or twice a day, either paddling the bright craft silently along the rocky shore or drifting like a brilliantly coloured bird on his sailboard. Occasionally, he would flash past in his small motor-boat, and once or twice, while out in her own canoe, she had seen him swimming near the island where he had his own cottage. But she had never approached him. Drawn though she was by the magnetism that increased each time she saw him, she could only wait for him to come to her.

And it seemed that this was the last thing he intended. Still seared by the contempt that had been in his eyes as he'd looked at her in the cottage, Laurie did not think he would ever come near her again. Common sense told her that he had probably left the lake. He was a busy man with a law practice to attend to. He had simply left after a few days out here, to go back to work.

All the same, she found her eyes continually drawn to the lake. Several times she paddled her canoe out beyond the bay, passing his island. Her eyes searched the clustering trees for a glimpse of his cottage, the shore for his canoe or motor-boat. She listened for any sound that might betray his presence.

But there was nothing to be seen or heard. The island seemed to be quite empty.

After a few days, Laurie decided to go shopping at the small town at the head of the lake. It was little more than a village, really, with a jetty where people moored their boats, a couple of stores and a craft shop which sold lunches and teas. Laurie had been there often with her parents. She decided to take the canoe rather than the motor-boat, although it was a long way to paddle. She would have lunch there and take it easy, making a day of it.

The end of the lake was more populated than Laurie's end. Many of the people who lived in the village worked at Kingston, something less than an hour's drive away, or at one of the smaller towns. There were also a good many cottages around the shore, some occupied all the year round, others used for holidays. At weekends, the village bustled with both cottagers and day-trippers, but today it was quiet.

Laurie moored her canoe with some relief. The journey had been a long one, more tiring that she had anticipated. Her arms and back ached from the paddling. She climbed out and strolled over to the craft shop for a coffee before beginning her shopping.

It had not occurred to her that she would be recognised—it was seventeen years since she had been here, a pigtailed child with gappy teeth. But she had reckoned without the country person's interest in the 'neighbours'—even those who lived several miles away down the lake—and the fact that her uncle's canoe was well-known and certain to be recognised.

'Why, you must be old Tom's niece!' the woman in the craft shop exclaimed as Laurie gave her order. 'Living here for a while, I hear. And weren't you the little girl whose mum and dad had that terrible accident all those years ago? Dreadful, that was, dreadful.' Her eyes were bright with curiosity. 'Went away somewhere, didn't you?'

'That's right.' Laurie tried not to show how much she disliked this inquisition. 'I lived with my uncle and aunt in Ottawa.'

'That's right. I remember old Tom telling me. Talked a lot about you, he did. Always hoped you'd come out and see him.' She poured Laurie's coffee and set a glass of iced water beside it. 'Well, he'd be glad to know you were here now, I know that.'

She turned away to serve another customer, and Laurie felt the familiar guilt wash over her. Why *hadn't* she come to see her uncle? Why hadn't she contacted the Brandons? She must have known they would welcome her. Why had she never done it?

John and Ella Marchant had made it difficult, she knew. Indeed, for a small child, still shocked by the loss of her parents, it had been impossible. How could she make telephone calls, write or receive letters without their help, without their knowledge? And she knew that they had felt it better that she should make a complete break with the past.

But why? Why had they felt that? Was it really because they had believed the contact would upset her? Or because they had disapproved of her parents so much that they had deliberately tried to kill their memory by cutting her off from all that she might associate with them?

Laurie finished her coffee and left the craft shop, smiling a goodbye at the woman who had served her. She did her shopping, buying some rolls to eat on the way back; somehow, she didn't feel like staying any longer in the village, where she might be recognised by someone else and subjected to a similar inquisition.

'Got far to go?' asked an old man on the jetty as she untied the rope fastening her canoe to a bollard. He nodded at the sky. 'Better get there fast. Storm blowing up, see.'

Laurie hesitated. She looked at the sky over the far end of the lake. There was no heavy cloud, just a thickening of the haze, a steely look that was reflected in the water.

'Oh, I can get home before that does anything,' she said cheerfully, and stepped into the canoe.

She paddled away, refreshed by the walk and the coffee. The sun beat down, hotter than ever, and she found a straw hat and put it on, shading her face.

Near the village, the lake was busy with people in hired boats, children in dinghies and shoppers like herself from other cottages. But after a while she found herself alone once more, moving steadily through the clear water, keeping close to the shore.

After a while she reached the group of islands, where the osprey nested in a tall tree, where she had come as a child with Russ and his brothers and sisters. She remembered the camps they had made, cooking the fish they had caught, swimming in tiny coves they thought of as their own, and she recalled too the games they had played, imagining themselves marooned on desert islands, battling with savages, pirates—always some new game, always something to catch their imagination.

It all seemed a long time ago. Like some other world, where everything was innocent and clear, where nothing terrible ever happened.

But terrible things did happen, even on a lake like this, so calm and peaceful. Terrible things that it was best, Aunt Ella had told her, not to think about, not to remember.

A sudden breeze ruffled the water and touched her face. Laurie looked up and saw that the haze had thickened now to real cloud. It hung above her, almost black, a brilliant white at the edges as it moved slowly beneath the sun and blotted it out. The lake turned dark, its sparkling gaiety disappearing into a sombre threat. She felt chilled and a little afraid.

But that was nonsense. She was over halfway back now. She would surely have time to reach home before the storm broke. All she needed to do was paddle faster. She had been taking it altogether too slowly.

Her plan to stop at one of the islands for lunch would have to be abandoned.

Laurie dug her paddle into the water, driving the canoe through the water. The breeze was stronger now, holding her back, and she fought it, setting up a small bow wave round the nose of the canoe. The heat had gone from the day, and the air struck cold on her bare arms. There was a brief flash of lightning and a distant mutter of thunder.

Laurie began to feel a little scared. To be out in a canoe in the middle of a lake during a thunderstorm was not the safest place. She glanced around, wondering where she could go for shelter. The shores of the lake at this point were rocky and inhospitable. There were no cottages for several miles, and where the shore itself was accessible it was thickly wooded, with tangled undergrowth reaching down to the water's edge. There were only the islands, strung like green jewels down the middle of the lake, and, in spite of her childhood games and fantasies, Laurie did not relish the idea of being stranded on one of them.

But there was one island that was inhabited. Russ's island. His cottage was there, and could provide shelter of a sort, even if it was locked. And Laurie knew that many people didn't bother to lock their cottages when they were away from them. Was Russ as casual as that?

Another flash of lightning, followed quickly by a much louder crack of thunder, decided her. She turned the canoe to head for Russ's island. And, as she did so, the first few drops of rain, large as pennies, fell from the sky and soaked her thin shirt.

*   *   *

The jetty was almost hidden in a tiny harbour, enclosed by two narrow reefs of rock, the water dark and deep between them. Laurie let her canoe drift in, and grasped at one of the posts to bring it close enough for her to step ashore. She moored it securely, then picked up her box of shopping and walked up the path that twisted through the trees.

There was no sign of Russ, no boat moored in the little cove. The island was silent save for the lashing of heavy rain. No birds sang; it was as if every creature had taken shelter.

Laurie felt the rain run down her body as if she were in a shower. Her hair hung against her neck and shoulders, soaked through. Her shirt and shorts clung to her skin, and she felt she might have been more comfortable if she were naked. The lightning was flashing almost continuously now, the thunder snapping and snarling like an angry watch-dog. She glanced anxiously at the trees as she hurried along, wondering which was the tallest. An island must be extra-vulnerable.

The path led her to a clearing, where the cottage stood overlooking the lake yet hidden from it by a tracery of birch trees. Built on a terrace of rocks, it was bigger than Laurie's cottage, with an attractive porch that stood high above the lawn. Rock steps led up to the porch, and Laurie climbed them slowly, suddenly aware of how weary she was, how wet and cold. Of course Russ wouldn't have left it unlocked, she thought. All the same, she tried the door.

To her utter astonishment, it swung open. And she found herself standing, for the first time, on Russ's threshold. With beating heart, almost afraid to go in, Laurie stepped inside. Instantly, out of the rain, shut away from the lightning, she felt better. She closed the door and looked around.

What had she expected from Russ's island home? Luxury, as in his office in Ottawa? Spartan living, with only the bare essentials? She wasn't sure. But what she saw took her by surprise.

A big room, with a kitchen at one end and a huge fireplace at the other. A bright rug on the floor with comfortably shabby easy-chairs and a sofa arranged around it. A low table, bookshelves filled with books and a clutter of maps and bits and pieces from boats and fishing tackle. A pile of boxes filled with games and puzzles—the kind of things all cottages had for bad weather.

An ordinary lake cottage, in fact—comfortable, undemanding, welcoming. Very like her own. A place where she could feel instantly at home.

Why hadn't she expected this? Why should it come as a surprise? Why had she got so muddled in her mind over Russ, and begun to see him as someone other than the boy who had shared her childhood, the boy with the friendly grin who had taught her to swim? Why had she begun to see him as some kind of different species—as a threat?

Laurie shook her head and realised suddenly just how wet she was. She must get out of these soaked clothes, find a towel and something else to put on. She must make a hot drink.

There wouldn't be any hot water, but she could light the fire—there was a large basket of logs standing by the hearth and a fire already laid. She found matches and lit the paper and twigs, watching as the flames licked up to the bigger sticks and logs. The warmth spread towards her. She found the cupboard where

Russ kept his towels, and chose a large one that was as blue as his eyes. Going back to the fire, she stripped off all her wet clothes, then wrapped herself in a blanket and sat before the flames, absorbing their warmth. Feeling suddenly exhausted, she pulled some cushions from the chairs and piled them on the floor, settling herself back against them as the storm raged outside and the room grew slowly darker.

Her eyes closed. She dozed and then slept. And when she woke again, it was to find the room completely dark, the fire died to a smouldering glow, and someone standing over her—a tall, dark shadow with eyes that gleamed as they looked down upon her nakedness.

CHAPTER SIX

LAURIE lay perfectly still, blinking slowly as she tried to remember where she was, how she had come here. The tall figure loomed menacingly above her, and fear crawled along her spine. She dared not move, filled with a superstitious dread that, if she did, the man would move too. And she knew herself to be powerless against him.

A chill struck her skin, and she realised that the blanket had fallen away from her body, leaving her exposed to his gaze in the dull red glow of the fire's embers. And now she knew where she was—on Russ's island, in his cottage, where she had no right to be.

And in the same instant she knew that this was Russ himself. But her fear did not flee; it merely took another direction.

'What on earth,' Russ asked, and the quietness of his tone was more frightening than any loud demand, 'are you doing here?'

Laurie pulled the blanket closely around her and sat up slowly, her eyes fixed on the shadowed face. 'I ran into the storm. I needed shelter.'

'So you chose my island to shelter on.' His voice was grim, as if he did not believe her. 'How very convenient. And how did you get in?'

'You left the door unlocked,' Laurie retorted, and felt a spark of satisfaction as he looked taken aback. 'You ought to take better care of your property if you don't want intruders.'

He looked as if he might challenge her assertion, then thought better of it. 'So you found it easy enough to get in. Well, no doubt I would have let you in if I'd been here, so I won't argue about that. But I'd just like to know who it is you've got on your side.'

'Who——?' Laurie shook her head, baffled. 'What are you talking about?'

'Up there, in the weather department. Arranging a storm to blow up when you were so conveniently close. Or maybe you were planning a visit anyway?'

'I most certainly was not!' Laurie would have liked to stand up and face him, but the blanket felt very insecure around her. 'Why, I haven't seen you for days—I thought you were away.'

'Exactly,' he said, and his tone was so dry that she caught her breath.

'Are you implying that you think I came here knowing you were away?'

'Well, didn't you?'

'I came for shelter,' she said tightly. 'I didn't know whether you were here or not, but I needed to get off the lake and I needed to find somewhere dry. I didn't think you'd object to my coming in when I found the door was unlocked, or to my lighting a fire——'

'But of course I don't. Why not bring some friends—throw a party? It seems a pity not to take the opportunity, don't you think?' He paused, watching her as if to gauge the effect of his sarcasm. 'Better still, why not invite your fiancé and his friend the land developer? Or will they be satisfied with your report?'

'My—report?'

'Yes. You'll want to see over the place, of course, get an idea of its true potential. Take a few measurements, that sort of thing. I may be able to help you there. I wouldn't like you to get anything wrong, after all.'

Laurie forgot her fears about the blanket. She scrambled to her feet, clutching it about her. She still had to look up at him, but at least she was on her feet now. She flung back her head and felt her hair, still damp, whisper across her bare shoulders.

'Look, Russ, I don't know what ideas you've got in your head about me——'

'Don't you?' he murmured, his glance moving slowly over her flushed face, her neck, and the breasts, tanned to a golden brown, which were only half covered by the rough blanket. 'Do you know, you look quite bewitching in—or rather, not quite in—that ravishing attire, Laurie?'

'No, I don't know! And don't try to distract me by behaving like a—a *man*!' she cried, and bit her lip in fury as he laughed. 'Oh, you *know* what I mean! You can't think of me like that—we knew each other as children——'

'A long time ago,' he said. 'And you've grown up quite a lot since then, Laurie.'

'Yes. I have. I've grown up enough to know when someone's making a pass at me to suit his own purposes.' She saw him begin to smile again, and stamped her foot uselessly, the bare sole making no sound at all on the thick rug. 'All right, so men always make passes to suit their own purposes—but at least they're generally honest enough to make it clear what they want. I don't know why you're doing it, Russ, but it isn't for the usual reason.'

'No? Well, let's say that I was just trying to defuse the situation a bit—take the heat out of it. You're getting all steamed up over nothing, Laurie. I know quite well why you're here and what you hope to achieve. And, since we're talking about honesty, why not be honest yourself and admit the truth?'

'The truth being...?'

'Why, that you and your smooth-talking fiancé intend to develop this lake to within an inch of its life, and want my island to be a part of your glitzy scheme. You thought I was away, and took the opportunity of coming to have a look—and the storm made a good excuse to come into the house. I admit I was a fool to leave the place unlocked, but we don't get intruders around here much. I hadn't reckoned on how quickly corruption can spread once it gets a foot in the door.'

Laurie gasped. ' "*Corruption*"? Why, that's a foul thing to say!'

'And what else would you call it?' he asked. 'Once money gets ideas, all decency goes out of the window. And that's all you and your precious fiancé are interested in—money. Never mind the scenic beauty you'll destroy, never mind the wildlife that will be lost. Never mind the peace that people come to these lakes to find, never mind the simple enjoyments and pleasures to be had here. No, you'll bring smart cars and leisure facilities, glossy people with glossy lifestyles, and the lake will be a different place. The loons will go, and the loons are the symbol of lakes like this. But where will they find enough peace to swim and fish and call across the water?' He paused, and Laurie heard the throb in his voice as he asked quietly, 'Don't you call that corruption?'

She stood silent for a moment. Then she lifted the blanket higher around her body, holding it above her shoulders, around her chin. She looked up into the dark face, her eyes wide, green as a cat's in the firelight.

'Yes,' she said. 'I do. And I've never—*never*—been in agreement with Alec over this. I've never been a party to his plans. None of that is ever going to happen, Russ.'

She stared into his eyes, willing him to believe her. But his face was filled with that searing contempt she dreaded, and his lip curled in disgust.

'You expect me to believe that? When I saw with my own eyes and heard the pair of you and that developer discussing your plans? Laurie, give me credit for a little sense, please. That man Morrison is well-known for his slippery deviousness over these matters. If he and your precious fiancé decide to put a time-share development or a theme park or a new Disneyland on this lake, it'll take World War Three to stop them. Not that that would deter me from doing it,' he added grimly. 'I've tangled with friend Morrison before—or maybe he didn't tell you that?'

Laurie stared at him. 'Morrison? No—I've tried to tell you, I'd never met him before that day. Russ, do you mean you've met him before?'

'On paper, yes. Not in the flesh—not that *that* was any loss. But he was behind another development— a few hundred miles away from here, but pretty similar. Nice, peaceful lake, full of wildlife, just a few cottagers content to live the simple life for a few weekends each year, one or two all-year-rounders, everyone happy—and then along came Morrison and some get-rich-quick merchant like your Alec, and slapped in plans to change it all. And boy, did they want change! They very nearly got it, too.'

'What happened?'

Russ grinned. 'They reckoned without an old guy who lived on the fringe of the lake. He'd been there since the year dot, before people began to think much about cottages. He didn't mind the odd few people coming, so long as they didn't disturb the loons or take too many fish, but he drew the line at what Morrison was planning. And he happened to be a friend of mine, so he asked me what he could do about it.'

'And?'

'Oh, we just got everyone together and opposed it,' Russ said casually. 'Morrison realised he wasn't going to win, and he withdrew. Not very gracefully, but he saw the sense of it, and that was that. I didn't imagine it was the last we'd seen of him—that kind of scum always does float to the surface again somewhere. But I didn't expect it to be *here*—and brought in by you!'

Laurie shook her head. 'Russ, I've told you——'

'I know what you've told me.' Russ's eyes were on her face, hard and disbelieving. 'I also know that Morrison will fight with any weapons he has to hand. Are you one of his weapons, Laurie? Did he send you here to try some other form of persuasion?'

'Some other——?' She stared up at him, trying to read the expression on the lean, shadowed face. He stepped a little closer and reached out one hand, laying his fingers on the edge of the blanket she clutched so tightly. Before she could move, he twitched it away from her shoulders and, as Laurie tried to retain it, she felt it slip even further, revealing her breasts to his gaze.

Russ came closer. She could feel the heat of him, radiating from his skin. His hands were warm on her shoulders, his fingers spread on her skin, his thumbs gently caressing the base of her neck.

'Is this what he sent you to do?' he muttered, his face so close to hers that she could feel the shape of the words on her skin. 'Is this what that oily businessman wants a wife for: to drive other men mad, so that they'll agree to anything for the sake of a kiss or two—or maybe more?'

He bent his head and touched her lips with his. Then, with a groan, he caught her hard against him, his mouth fierce on hers. Laurie drew her breath in with a gasp and as her lips parted she felt his tongue force its way between them, thrusting, seeking, probing. She lifted a hand in weak protest, then let it fall limply back to her side. Her senses reeled and she was conscious only of Russ's lips on hers, his tongue meeting and mingling with hers, his hands on her body and his hardness against her.

He was holding her close now, one arm hard around her waist, his hand reaching up to splay across her shoulder-blade. She felt his other hand slide down the length of her neck to her breast and cover it, his palm slightly rough against the softness of her skin. His fingers touched her nipple; he began to tease it between finger and thumb, and Laurie felt it harden under his touch. His mouth was still on hers, his tongue probing, withdrawing, probing deeply again, his lips shaping hers so that she could not escape. Nor could she try; the weakness that had invaded her with his first touch had spread now over all her body, so that she could barely stand, and she felt him recognise this and hold her more firmly against him before he lowered her to the rug before the dying fire, and lay down beside her, his free hand straying now over her body, sliding under the blanket to explore her hips, her thighs, her belly.

Laurie sighed and moved in his arms. The first violence of his onslaught had gentled now, and she felt like a cat being stroked and caressed into purring ecstasy by a loving owner.

Russ's mouth moved away from hers and he began to plant swift, tiny kisses all over her face. Laurie turned her head, trying to find his mouth again with her own, but he evaded her and his lips slid down her neck, found the tender spot between her breasts and then moved to enfold her nipple. She felt the quick movements of his tongue against the trembling flesh and, at the same moment, his fingertips brush the thin, sensitive skin of her thighs, and she twisted against him, wanting suddenly to feel his skin against hers, his body wholly against her.

As if making an effort, Russ lifted himself away from her. She stared up at him, her eyes dark, waiting in the near-darkness for the feel of him; but he moved away. She felt his hands fumble with the blanket, then found herself covered again. A moment later the light snapped on, and she shrank from its cruel glare.

'Russ——?'

He stood tall, looking down at her, his face expressionless. But the contempt was back in his voice as he said, 'So I was right. You did come here for that. My God, Laurie, what have you become? What is it worth to you, to get your way over this? And what sort of man is it you're planning to marry, if he can ask this of you?'

Laurie sat up, shuddering, unable to believe what she was hearing. There was a bitterness in Russ's voice that seemed to come from more than contempt, from some deeper emotion. As if what had happened had been an assault on him, rather than . . .

With a swift wave of revelation, she realised just what had been happening. Russ hadn't wanted to make love to her at all. He had been testing her, testing a theory that she had come here to seduce him, to coax him with her body into selling them his property, his island. And her reactions had convinced him that he was right.

He would never believe that his touch had been enough to set her on fire, that his kiss had shaken her to her soul, that his caresses had roused such an urgent longing in her. He would never believe that she would have been too weak to resist him if he had continued, that even now her body was quivering with the need he had evoked.

Shame broke over her like an ocean-roller. She bowed her head. How could she have reacted like that? She had been ready to give herself to Russ, at no more than a touch! What had possessed her?

She stood up slowly, holding the blanket around her as if it were a shield. Still trembling, she faced him and tried to recover her shattered dignity. 'You're wrong,' she said in a shaking voice. 'I didn't come here for that, or for anything to do with your precious island. I don't *want* it—but I'd obviously be wasting my time expecting you to believe it. And I don't intend to develop the lake or allow Alec to do so, but I shan't expect you to believe that either. You're determined, for some reason only you can know, to think the worst of me. And now I think I'll go. If you don't mind.'

Russ's eyes were dark as sapphires. He looked at her coldly, then, unbelievably, shook his head.

'Oh, but I do mind,' he said softly. 'For one thing, the weather's still pretty bad out there. And it's almost dark. You couldn't possibly go out in your canoe now. And besides—you and I haven't finished with each other yet.' He came close again, lifting his hand, and ran one finger down her body, from throat to waist. He watched as Laurie closed her eyes, trying not to shiver, and she knew that he felt the tremor she could not repress. She saw the smile on his face, and shrank inside.

'You can't keep me here,' she whispered, and he laughed softly.

'No? Well, we'll see about that—shan't we? And now we'd better think about a meal. We don't need to starve, do we? I see you brought some provisions—very thoughtful of you. And I've plenty in store too—we should be able to hold out for quite a long time.'

Laurie took a step forward. Her heart was thumping now with fear and anger. She felt the blanket slip, and took a fresh grip on it.

'I won't stay. You can't keep me; it's kidnapping—it's against the law!'

'I do know the law,' he said in an amused tone. 'I make my living by it, remember?' He picked up the still damp clothes that Laurie had discarded earlier. 'I'll take care of these. You won't be wanting them for a while. And I don't think you're likely to try to get away wearing nothing but a rather cumbersome and—if I may say so—delightfully revealing blanket. Are you?'

Laurie opened her mouth, but no words came. She watched helplessly as he bundled her clothes under his arm and moved, whistling cheerfully, towards the door. She took a step to follow him, and tripped over the trailing end of the blanket.

Russ looked back and grinned.

'Nuisance, isn't it?' he said sympathetically. 'I should think you wish you'd never come here, don't you?' His grin faded. 'But not as much as you're going to wish it, Laurie, my sweet,' he added softly. 'Not nearly as much as you're going to wish it...'

Laurie crouched for a while by the dying fire, then threw on another log. If she was to be incarcerated here, she might as well be warm. She wondered where Russ had gone. Surely he hadn't left the island and abandoned her? He wouldn't...would he?

She got up and went to peer out of the window. It was quite dark now, but she could hear the rain lashing against the glass, and shivered. It wasn't really cold, but the change in the weather, breaking the steady heat that she had grown accustomed to, made it seem chilly, even with the fire. She turned away from the window.

Russ must be somewhere around, but in any case there was no reason why she shouldn't explore the cottage and find out where everything was. Anyway, she needed to find the bathroom. She went up the stairs and found herself on a wide landing with several doors opening from it.

The cottage was quite a lot bigger than hers, and Laurie guessed that there were probably three or four bedrooms. Cautiously, she began to open the doors. The first was evidently used as an office; there were a desk, two filing cabinets and a large bookcase in it. On the desk stood a computer and a telephone.

A telephone! Laurie stepped towards it, reaching out. Then she drew back her hand. Whom could she telephone for help? Her aunt and uncle in Ottawa? Alec, in Toronto? The *police*? Each was equally impossible. Her uncle and aunt simply wouldn't believe that Russ Brandon was holding her hostage on an island in the middle of the lake. Neither would the police. And Alec—well, hadn't she told him that she never wanted to see him again? How could she beg for help from him?

Dispiritedly, Laurie turned away. She tried the next door, and found it was a bathroom. She went inside and locked the door. It was a temptation to stay in there, putting herself under siege, but she realised that it would do no good—she would have to come out some time, and would only humiliate herself further. She did not intend to starve simply in order to annoy Russ Brandon!

What were the other rooms? She opened another door and peeped in, half afraid that she would find Russ himself in there. But there was nobody. Laurie slipped through the door and closed it behind her.

And felt, for a moment, as if she had strayed into the lair of some great jungle animal.

The room was dominated by a huge double bed—more than king-size, she thought, staring at it. It was covered by a thick, shaggy rug that looked like the skin of a gigantic tiger, striped in black and gold. Laurie touched it tentatively and was relieved to find that it was fake—she had half expected it to attack her. Almost reluctantly, she took her eyes from it and looked around the rest of the room.

It was quite clearly Russ's own room, furnished to his taste. It was a mixture of the exotic and the spartan—the bed was the only luxury in the room; apart from that there was little furniture, merely a built-in cupboard and chest of drawers, a chair and, by the window, a table with various items of personal belongings scattered on it.

The wooden walls of the room were hung with pictures—some of them paintings of the lake in all its moods, some photographs. The loons were there, both in paint and on film, their black and white striped necks rising from the water in stark silhouette. The heron was there, standing motionless on a sandy beach just as she had seen him stand in her own little bay. The osprey was there, soaring high to its nest in a tall tree, and again swooping down to catch a fish, its huge wings beating the water into a foam.

In one corner, a pair of skis leaned against the wall, with ice-skates on the floor beneath them. A fishing-rod occupied another corner, and near by she saw an easel and paints. There was a half-finished picture on the easel, and Laurie moved to look at it.

A sound from downstairs jerked her to attention, and she realised that Russ was unlikely to be pleased to find her poking about in his room. Hurriedly, she backed out, and as she heard him coming up the stairs she dived through the next door and found herself in another bedroom.

This room was quite different from Russ's. It held twin beds, each covered with a bright patchwork quilt. On the wall hung cheerful, 'cottagey' prints, and the floor was covered with a colourful rug. Clearly, this room was for guests, and had been decorated to extend a welcome.

Laurie felt unhappy as she stood there, wishing that the welcome could have been extended to her. But she was here uninvited. And although Russ had declared his intention of keeping her here, it wasn't for the pleasure of her company—he had made that very clear.

'So you're finding your way about.' He was behind her, his voice and face expressionless. What was he thinking behind those cold blue eyes? she wondered. 'Well, you may as well. This is where you'll be sleeping, after all. I'd rather you didn't go exploring in the other bedrooms, however.'

'Why not? Do you keep all your wives in there, like Bluebeard?' she asked with a flippancy she didn't feel. And Russ didn't seem to find her remark funny either.

'I don't have any wives. Marriage is something I haven't experimented with so far.' His voice was clipped. He turned away. 'Come downstairs now, Laurie. I've brought in some more logs for the fire, and started cooking a meal. You can help.'

'No "please"?' she asked as she followed him.

He turned on the stairs to face her, and she realised that even though he stood two steps below her she still had to look up to meet his eyes.

'No. No "please". You're not here as a guest, Laurie. You came of your own volition, and while you're here——'

'Which is *not* of my own volition,' she broke in angrily, forgetting her own similar thoughts of a few moments ago.

'—while you're here you'll do as I say. And I'd like you to make some salad now, while I cook the steaks.'

'And if I don't?'

'I only cook one steak,' he returned imperturbably. 'And I can quite easily make my own salad.'

Laurie was defeated. She couldn't even say she didn't want anything to eat—she was already hungry, and would be even hungrier by morning if she ate nothing now. And Russ was, she knew, quite capable of eating his own meal while she sat by eating nothing. It was her choice.

'Well, I'll need some proper clothes,' she said, indicating the blanket she still held around herself. 'I can't do anything with this thing on.'

'Oh, we'll soon fix that. There are some safety-pins here somewhere.' He went across to the kitchen end of the big room and rummaged in a drawer. 'Yes, I thought so. Come here and I'll fix it for you.'

'I'll fix it for myself, thank you very much.'

'Try, then.' He handed her the pins and Laurie struggled to fasten the blanket around her tightly enough to prevent it slipping. After a few moments, during which she grew redder and hotter and more and more flustered under his sardonic gaze, she threw him a murderous glare and handed him the pins.

'All right. You do it. But don't——'

'Don't what?' he said softly, standing close to her as he pinned the blanket together. 'Don't kiss you again? Why not, Laurie? Why don't you want me to kiss you? Isn't it what you came here for?' He stood very close, looking into her eyes, and then he moved slowly nearer. His lips brushed hers, and Laurie shivered. 'Isn't it what you want?' he breathed, and she felt the movement of his mouth against hers. His tongue flicked very lightly across her lips, and she gave a tiny moan and closed her eyes.

There was a brief silence. Then she became aware that Russ was no longer close to her. She opened her eyes again to find him watching her with an expression she didn't want to read.

'There's a name for women like you, Laurie,' he said quietly. 'Whether they do it for money or for—other reasons. And it isn't a very flattering name.'

As Laurie gasped, he turned away. He went to the kitchen bench and stared down at the plates he had set out there, the steaks waiting to be grilled, the salad ready to be made. 'I find I'm not very hungry after all,' he told her harshly. 'Cook yourself something if you want. I'm taking some bread and cheese to my study—I've got work to do.' And he gathered his meal together quickly and disappeared without a further glance.

Laurie stood in silence, burning with humiliation. How dared he talk to her like that? How dared he insinuate...? But she knew that it wouldn't have been nearly so bad if her own reactions had been different. If she had been able to resist his touch, his kiss. If she hadn't *wanted* it so much...

Why did he have such an effect on her? What was it about him—when she didn't even like him any more? She thought regretfully of the Russ of her childhood, the laughing teenager who had swung her on to his shoulders, held her safely while she learned to swim, taught her to sail, to row, to paddle a canoe. What had happened to turn him into this hard-eyed man who could set her alight with a touch, yet shrivel her with a glance?

The storm died out towards morning, and Laurie woke to find sunshine flooding in through the window, lighting up the colours on the patchwork quilt so that they glowed like stained glass. She lay for a few moments, looking around the room, thinking how pleasant it was, and trying once more to equate it with the man who was keeping her here against her will.

But need she stay here any longer? The lake was calm again now; there was nothing to stop her taking her canoe and paddling back down the lake to her own bay. Russ would not dare to come and kidnap her from there—and why should he want to anyway? And, if he was still asleep, this might be her only chance.

Quickly, Laurie slipped out of bed, then remembered that she had no clothes. Russ had taken hers away, and she had no idea where she could find any others. She could wear the blanket again, but it was difficult to pin it securely enough herself, and it would be cumbersome and awkward in the canoe.

She opened the cupboard, but it was empty. Frowning, she turned to survey the room. A pillowcase? She stripped one from one of the pillows and held it up against herself. No—it was far too short, and in any case she would have to damage it. Not that she had any scruples about that, she told herself staunchly; but she dropped the pillowcase and looked again at the bed.

A sheet. She pulled off the top sheet and wrapped it around her body like a toga. It was too long, but easier to pin, and she gathered up the long ends and tied them over one shoulder. She had no shoes, and would have to go barefoot; she hoped the path to the harbour wasn't stony.

There was still no sound from Russ's room. Quietly, with infinite care, Laurie opened her door and crept out on to the landing. Did the stairs creak? She had no idea, could only take each one with slow, heart-thumping care and hope for the best. Very, very cautiously, expecting at every moment to hear Russ come out of his room, she tiptoed down towards the big living-room.

Suppose he wasn't in his room at all? Suppose he was down here already, listening to her, watching with that sardonic smile, waiting for her to see him? Laurie looked around the room as she descended, and breathed a sigh of relief to find it empty. But that didn't mean he was still asleep. He could be outside...

She would not feel safe until she was in her canoe—and not even then, she thought with a sick feeling. He could pursue her in his motor-boat, drag her back... For heaven's sake! She was talking about piracy! People didn't *do* that sort of thing—did they?

People didn't kidnap grown women and keep them on lonely islands either. But Russ had done just that.

In the broad light of day, it seemed crazy. He couldn't have meant it. He must have been joking—or just trying to frighten her. He couldn't mean to keep her here. It was ridiculous.

Feeling bolder now, Laurie slipped out through the door and ran down the porch steps. The island lay beneath her, sparkling with the rain that had not yet dried in the sun. Droplets hung in the trees, catching the light and flashing like a necklace of diamonds. Beyond the trees the lake lay blue and innocent, as if it had never been whipped up into a dark, angry maelstrom and threatened to overturn her canoe. Far out, she could see the dark head and neck of a loon, swimming low in the water, its big, dark body almost submerged.

How could Russ believe that she would want to spoil all this?

Laurie picked her way down the path towards the little harbour. It was mostly grass, but the odd stone and root from a tree made her walk carefully, and she could not go as quickly as she longed to. She looked over her shoulder, fearful still of being followed. But there was no one in sight.

The path dipped into a little valley that hid her from the house, then twisted behind some rocks. Laurie took a deep, quivering breath. She was out of sight at last—she could hurry. And she quickened her pace, anxious only to be away from here, off the island, safe back in her own domain.

A thin green snake slid suddenly across her path, making her jump back. But it was harmless, and she went on quickly, her heart hammering. Even now Russ might have woken to find her missing, might be coming down the path in pursuit. He wouldn't—surely wouldn't—take her back by force? But, if he chose to do that, what could she do to stop him? He was taller, bigger, heavier, stronger than she. She would be utterly powerless.

Just as she had been when he'd held her in his arms and kissed her.

Laurie felt a tingle deep in her body; its sharpness left her gasping. She stopped for a moment, resting against a tree, shaken by the memory of the kisses, the caresses, the sensations that had stormed through her body at his touch. Once again she wondered at the effect this man could have on her, an effect no other man had ever had. Not even Alec, the man she had once promised to marry.

Especially not Alec . . .

A sound broke the stillness. Laurie lifted her head sharply, listening for it to be repeated. Had it been a twig cracking under the tread of a foot? Her heart kicked and she ran on quickly, hardly noticing the roughness of the path beneath her feet. Surely she must be almost at the harbour?

The path twisted once more and she was there. The rocks ran out in two dark reefs on either side of the deep, narrow channel. There was the jetty, built along the side of one of the reefs, with room for several boats to be moored against it.

And there was nothing. No canoe. No motor-boat such as Russ must have come in yesterday. Nothing.

Laurie stared unbelievingly. Where were they? Where was her canoe? Had it drifted away? Could she have fastened it carelessly in her hurry to escape the storm? But she knew that she hadn't. She had moored it tightly. It ought to have been here.

The truth dawned slowly in her mind, and she sank down on the beach, gazing at the empty harbour, hearing the little waves slap lightly against the rocks, knowing now that there was no escape.

Russ had removed her canoe. He had come down here before she woke, and taken her little craft away, knowing that she would try to escape. Perhaps he had left the island altogether.

But why? Why should he want to keep her a prisoner here?

CHAPTER SEVEN

A SPEAR of morning sunlight slid through the trees and touched the dark water of the harbour with brightness. Laurie, still staring at the empty space where her canoe had been, sat down on a flat rock and drew the sheet more closely around her body.

What did Russ mean to do with her? Why was he keeping her—what purpose could it possibly serve? For the first time, she wondered if he might be not quite sane. Surely no rational person would kidnap a woman and hold her prisoner for no reason?

No. He had a reason, of that she was sure. And she remembered the way he held her last night, the kisses he had given her, the way his hands had searched for the tender spots of her body, and shivered.

But he would have to be mad...

I can't go back, she thought suddenly. Whether Russ were still on the island, she had no idea—there was no boat here, but there could well be another harbour or jetty somewhere—but until she knew she dared not go back to the house. If he was there, waiting for her... The shiver became a shudder that shook her from head to toe.

So what was she to do? Roam about the island wrapped only in a sheet until someone came to call? And if they did—how could she approach anyone and ask for help? They would think it was she who was mad.

Laurie stared at the empty jetty. There must be another one somewhere. There must be another small cove or landing place on the island, where Russ kept the assortment of boats that all cottagers possessed— sailing dinghies, canoes, his motor-boat. If she could find that, she might be able to use one of them to get away. She might even find her own canoe.

Suddenly excited, she jumped up and stole cautiously up the path leading from the harbour. She didn't want to risk running into Russ now. She remembered that sound she had heard, as if someone had trodden on a twig. He might be watching her even now.

The thought brought a tingle to her spine, and she turned her head, trying to see through the thick bushes. But if anyone had been there, she could not have seen them. And why would Russ hide to watch her, anyway? He was more likely to come stalking down the path and grab her, using his greater strength to carry her back to the house. And then ... Again, her spine tingled and she shivered, feeling once more a whisper of the sensations his caresses had called up in her own body.

She must never allow that to happen again. For some reason, Russ could affect her in a way no other man had ever done. In his arms, she became helpless, unable to resist. And she dared not let herself become subject to him in that way again. It was too dangerous.

Once let Russ invade her body, and she would never be her own person again. Even her heart would be in peril ...

Suddenly panic-stricken, Laurie turned quickly away from that thought, and hurried along the path. She felt as if eyes were watching her from behind every tree, as if all her nerve-ends were standing out from her skin. Her bare feet stumbled painfully on the rough, stony path, and she clutched at the sheet that threatened to slip from her naked body. Anger touched her at the thought of her situation, so ridiculous, so humiliating—and so frightening. When I get away from here, she thought murderously, I'm going to make sure that Russ Brandon regrets this for the rest of his life.

Shortly after she left the harbour, Laurie saw that the path was crossed by another, the main track leading back to the cottage. This must be the path that led round the edge of the island. She hesitated, then turned left, since that seemed to be least likely to be seen from the house and, thankful to see that it led across grass rather than stones and rough earth, quickened her pace.

There was no doubt that the island was as near perfect as it was possible for an island to be. In other circumstances, Laurie would have revelled in exploring the smooth rocks, the soft, grassy clearings, the craggy little bays and promontories. She would have wandered under the trees, delighting in the dappled sunlight that made patterns on the turf, watching the many birds that flew and sang above her head. She would have sat happily on the little headlands, gazing dreamily out over the lake, watching the change in its moods, seeing the light change from the hard brightness of noon, through the softer glow of late afternoon, into the burnished glow of the sunset.

She could, in fact, have been very happy here.

Laurie walked on, conscious of a sadness weighing on her heart. A sadness she couldn't quite analyse.

There had never, after all, been any question of her living here. She had her own cottage anyway. And nothing had changed in her life—other than the breaking of her engagement to Alec, which she knew had been the right thing to do. Her job was still there for her to return to in the autumn, she had her flat in Toronto, her friends.

So why did she feel as if she had lost something important to her—something she had been within an inch of grasping, but never quite recognised?

Laurie turned a corner in the path, passed a large rock and stopped. She took a deep breath. She had found the other landing place.

Russ's motor-boat lay moored alongside a jetty that stood out from the rocks into the smooth waters of a small horseshoe-shaped cove. On the sandy beach was a sailboard, its mast and sail leaning against a nearby tree as if someone meant to use it soon. And there, pulled up on the shore, were two canoes— Laurie's and the bright orange one that she recognised as Russ's.

Laurie ran down to the beach, her heart thumping with excitement. Now she could escape! Now she could take her canoe and paddle away from this island, away from Russ. He couldn't stop her now.

She had run to her canoe, grasped its prow and begun to drag it into the water, when she realised that there was no paddle in it. Laurie stopped, her heart plummeting in dismay. She looked into Russ's canoe; there was no paddle there either. She cast desperate glances up and down the beach, but there was no sign of any paddle. And without a paddle, she could not hope to use the canoe, not for any distance.

Dispiritedly, she pulled the canoe back from the water, and stood thinking. The motor-boat. Would it be stealing if she took that? But even that would be no more crime than Russ's kidnapping and keeping her here against her will. And she wouldn't be keeping it. He could have it back—any time he cared to come and collect it.

She ran along the jetty, and looked down into the cockpit. But, as she might have known, there were no keys.

So that was that. Laurie turned away, more depressed now than she had ever been. Russ had made quite sure that she could not escape from the island. And he was still here himself—the presence of both the motor-boat and the canoe made that clear.

She couldn't go on hiding from him for ever. Eventually, he would either find her or she would be forced to give herself up.

Laurie stared despondently around. At the lake, so shining, so empty. At the island, with the roof of the cottage just visible above the trees. At the beach with its useless craft. At the sailboard.

The sailboard! Once again, her heart leapt. There it was, with its sail near by, all ready to be used. But could she manage it? Laurie had tried windsurfing once or twice before with Sue, in Toronto, and enjoyed it, though she had never managed to keep the board sailing for more than a few minutes. 'You have to fall in a hundred times before you can sail,' Sue had told her, and Laurie had grinned, and remarked that she reckoned she was two-thirds of the way there . . . But that had been a year ago, and she hadn't touched a sailboard since. Could she possibly manage this one, just enough to get her away from the island?

It wouldn't matter where she came ashore—she could find her way back to her own bay. It was worth trying anyway.

Quickly, Laurie went over to the sailboard and examined it. It looked rather more advanced than the model she had been lent, but perhaps that might make it easier to manage. She carried it to the water's edge, then went back for the sail.

Carrying that was more cumbersome, and fitting it to the sailboard, in a slightly different way from the one she had been shown, took her a few minutes to work out. She worked with trembling fingers, terrified that Russ would come and catch her before she could get into the water. And even then she wouldn't be safe... But at last she had the sail fixed and laid on the board, ready to be erected when she was out in open water.

Laurie floated the board out into the water until she could ease her body on to it without tipping it up. She sat astride, paddling with her hands, and the light craft moved slowly out across the lake.

It might be more sensible simply to do this, paddling with her hands to safety. But there was a light breeze blowing, just enough to carry her away swiftly. And a quick glance back at the island, with the cottage now more clearly in view, reminded her that Russ needed only to glance out of a window to see her there, and that he would be able to catch her within a few minutes in his motor-boat. She simply did not have time.

She would have to try to sail it. And it wasn't that difficult, after all. She knew what to do, she'd managed it several times, she could do it again. And the urgency of her situation would help—she simply wouldn't have *time* to make mistakes.

Carefully, Laurie let the sail droop into the water. The board drifted idly and she drew in her legs, then raised herself to a kneeling position. She caught hold of the curved 'wishbone' that enclosed the sail, and worked her hands along it, lifting herself slowly to a standing position as the sail too came upright out of the water.

There was a brief moment of struggle before she realised she was about to lose her balance. Then the board tipped, the sail dropped and Laurie fell headlong into the water with a resounding splash. As soon as she hit the water, she remembered that she was not wearing a life-jacket. She kicked her way to the surface, and caught at the board, which was floating just over her head. Spluttering, she dragged in a deep breath of air and rested for a second or two, wishing that there had been a life-jacket in one of the canoes, or the boat. She could swim strongly enough, but a life-jacket did bring you to the surface quickly when you fell in.

The sheet had slipped from her body entirely as she fell, and Laurie was acutely conscious of her nakedness as she scrambled back on to the sailboard. But she could not worry about that now—there was nothing to be done about it, and there was nobody here to see anyway. The lake was quite deserted. And a quick glance at the island showed no sign of life there either.

She clambered back on to the sailboard, half kneeling as she lifted the sail carefully from the water. That was the way—slowly, delicately, keeping the balance between herself, the sail and the board just right. Her bare feet stood firm on the matt surface, set wide apart, sensing every movement of the board on the shifting surface of the water. The 'wishbone' was steady in her hands, the sail lifting steadily. It was almost upright now, and the soft wind caught it, filling it firmly so that the board suddenly began to move. Laurie caught her breath, shifted her grip suddenly—and found herself falling once more into the deep water of the lake.

This time she sank further under the water, and had to kick hard to swim upwards towards the sunlight. She had fallen with the sail too, and found herself entangled in its bright folds. With a moment of panic, she lifted it clear, so that she could breathe before ducking underneath again to swim clear.

If only she had had a life-jacket...

For a third time, Laurie set herself on the board. Her heart was thumping, but she was determined to master it. It was her only chance of escaping Russ, after all. She *must* get away.

The sail came up, slowly, filled with air, and billowed tightly ahead of her. The board began to move, fast. Laurie felt a surge of exhilaration. She was sailing—she was really sailing. She hardly dared look up to see how fast she was moving, or even in which direction, but the water was surging past her now; there was even a small bow wave of white foam, and every second was taking her further away from the island, every second——

'*Watch it!* You're heading for the rocks!'

The voice burst in upon her consciousness, and she started and lost control of the sail. In another second it was over, and the board tipped Laurie headlong into the water. Once again she went through the struggle of thrusting herself up to the surface, emerging with her hair across her face. Breathlessly, she shook it back and looked around for the board.

It was floating close beside her. And holding it steady, sitting in a bright orange canoe, was Russ. Laurie stared at him. She was beginning to think she had strayed into a nightmare.

'Hi there,' he said cheerfully. 'Great morning for a sail. But you really ought to be wearing a life-jacket, you know.' His eyes moved over her body, slender and golden in the sunlit water, and he added, 'If nothing else.'

Laurie gasped and closed her eyes. What had she ever done that meant she had to be punished this way? 'You don't have to look,' she retorted angrily, but Russ only laughed.

'Why not, when you so clearly don't approve of clothes anyway? I seem to have seen you more often without them than with. Mind, you look pretty good when you do dress up, I'm ready to admit that—but just at the moment I'm not complaining.'

'Well, I am!' She moved round to the far side of the sailboard, though she knew that it was of little use to try to hide herself from him. And there was no escape anyway. She would have to go back to the island with him. 'Why don't you let me go?' she asked desperately. 'What possible good can it do to keep me here? You're going to have to in the end.'

'Certainly,' he agreed, smiling. 'But not until I've done my damnedest to persuade you of one or two things I happen to think are important.'

'What things, for heaven's sake? Russ, you still don't understand——'

'Then let's spend a little time finding out.' He pulled the sailboard nearer to the canoe, and Laurie found herself being swept along with it. She came within reach of the canoe and, before she could retreat, Russ leaned over and grasped her wrist.

'Well?' His face was very close to hers, his mouth smiling, his lake-blue eyes glinting. 'What do you want to do, Laurie—come with me on the canoe or ride the sailboard? It's your choice.'

Laurie looked up at him. She thought of the alternatives. Scrambling up on to the sailboard to ride it back to the island, towed by the canoe, her nakedness exposed to his gaze? Or being helped into the canoe, feeling his hands on her body again—she shivered—and closer than she ever wanted to be again?

'What do I want to do?' she asked slowly. 'Well, of the two, I think I'd prefer to do this...' And she reached up, slipped her arm around his neck and jerked sharply.

Taken completely off guard, Russ overbalanced, the canoe tipped sideways, and he fell headlong into the water, taking Laurie down with him into the depths of the lake. She felt his body hard against hers, arms and legs kicking as he fought his way to the surface again. Laurie came with him, choking but triumphant. For once, she had caught Russ by surprise, and, although she knew she had done herself no good by achieving it, she still enjoyed the feeling.

'Why, you little vixen!' he spluttered, and reached out a hand to catch her. Laurie ducked away, but Russ was too strong a swimmer for her to escape him. He caught her by the hair, and towed her back to where the canoe and the sailboard still drifted. The canoe had righted itself, and he swam to the stern and laid one hand on the coaming. Then he looked at her.

Their faces were very close in the water. Russ had an arm around Laurie's shoulders now and his hand was tight on her arm. She could feel the length of his body against hers, and realised with a shock that he wore only a pair of thin shorts. It was as if he were as naked as she, and the contact of skin against skin was like an electric shock.

Laurie raised her eyes and looked at him in appeal.

'Please,' she whispered, 'let me go.'

But Russ was staring at her. His expression had changed but she couldn't define it. The cobalt-blue of his eyes had darkened, the pupils widening until there was no more than a rim of bright blue encircling them. His arm shifted slightly, and the tips of his fingers slid round to touch the edge of her breast.

'Russ...' she breathed, and he pulled her closer and bent his head to lay his lips on hers.

Laurie felt her body float upwards to lie along the surface of the water. Her legs drifted into a wafting entanglement with his, and she felt the hardness of his muscles, the power of his thighs against her. Her lips parted under his and she felt his tongue invade her mouth, probing gently, touching her teeth with tiny, flickering movements, then coming in closer, deeper, to explore the softness that lay within. Her own tongue met it in a dance of twining, sliding joy, and as his retreated she followed it with her own, exploring in her turn. She was no longer aware of her surroundings, knew only that she was in Russ's arms in a delicious drift of enchantment, a floating heaven that held yet more delights. She felt his hand slide down her body, caressing her breasts, her waist, the softness of her thighs, and she whimpered with pleasure and swayed against him.

Russ took his mouth from hers slowly, reluctantly. He looked at her again, and Laurie gazed back, wanting him to kiss her again, wanting him to love her...

Sanity returned sharply. She twisted suddenly in his arms, kicked herself away from him. From a safe distance, she stared at him, brushing back her wet hair, breathing hard.

'Laurie——'

'No!' she gasped. 'No—don't touch me again, Russ. *Don't*. I'm not interested—do you understand?—not in you. And if your idea in keeping me here is to seduce me——'

'It's not,' he interrupted. His eyes were stormy. 'It never was.'

'Well, you could have fooled me. You've done your damnedest ever since you got me alone; you've kept my clothes from me, you've pawed me at every possible opportunity——'

'*Pawed* you?' he broke in. 'I hardly think that what I——'

'Yes, *pawed* me. You haven't left me alone for a second——'

'I left you alone all night. Don't you think that, if I'd really been intent on having my wicked way with you, you'd have been in my bed before midnight? Or I'd have been in yours? Laurie, let me assure you, if I really set out to seduce a woman——'

'Thank you, no,' she said coldly, treading water and keeping a safe distance from him. 'I'd rather not hear about your dubious methods.'

Russ stared at her, then broke into sudden laughter. Laurie watched in indignation until he stopped laughing and looked at her, his mouth twitching.

'What's so funny?' she asked suspiciously.

'Nothing. Everything. You—me. All this.' He waved his arm around them. 'Coming out to the middle of the lake to quarrel. Look—let's stop this and be sensible, Laurie. You must be cold, I know I am, and we need to get back and have a hot drink and get some food inside us. I'm going to get into the canoe, even if you're not. Ride the board, if you want to—I promise not to look. Though I don't know what you think I might see that I haven't had quite a good look at already!'

He scrambled back aboard the canoe, and Laurie, seeing the sense of his words, swam to the sailboard and wriggled back on to it. Russ, keeping his word, fastened the board to the canoe, and began to paddle towards the island, his back to her. When they arrived at the beach he pulled the canoe up on the sand and went over to the motor-boat.

'Here,' he said, glancing across to where Laurie was standing shoulder-deep in the water, holding the sailboard. 'Here's a towel. I'll leave it here and you can come out and wrap yourself in it. I'll be up at the cottage, getting some coffee going. You can come up and have a hot shower straight away.'

He turned without a glance and disappeared up the path. Laurie, aware of how cold she had become, came out of the water and picked up the towel. She rubbed herself dry, then wrapped it around herself. Making sure that the board was safely ashore, she followed Russ up the path.

She felt as exhausted as if she had lived through a week without sleep. Physically, the struggles with the sailboard had left her bruised and aching. Her arms and back ached from the paddling she had done yesterday. And she felt hollow with hunger.

But those discomforts were nothing compared with the emotional turmoil she felt. It was as if her heart had been torn from her breast, roughly manhandled, and then pushed back in and hastily covered up. As if her deepest feelings had been taken out, exposed to the ruthless glare of daylight, and trampled upon.

Yet at the same time it was as if she had been gently stroked with a finger that called for her love, her passion, that had needs of its own that she longed to meet.

And that was what she should most beware, Laurie thought. That was where the greatest peril lay—in Russ's ability to make her melt, to make her believe that she loved him—and believe it when she was in most danger, when she was in his arms.

She must never allow herself to be in his arms again. But how was she going to prevent it—kept here on an island, in close proximity, and without even clothes to protect her?

When she entered the kitchen, the damp towel clinging to her body, Laurie found Russ sliding a tray of buttered English muffins into the oven. The smell of fresh coffee filled the air, and she realised just how much she needed it. She stood at the door, half nervous, half defiant.

'Oh, hi,' Russ said as if she were a neighbour, dropping in on a casual visit. 'Coffee's just about ready. Why don't you pour yourself a mug and sit down?' He turned and glanced at her. 'Unless you'd rather get dressed first?' he added with the ghost of a smile.

' "Get dressed"?' Laurie repeated stupidly, as if he'd suggested half an hour's hang-gliding before breakfast.

'Mm. Dressed. You know—clothes, that kind of thing?' He was grinning openly now. 'Or maybe you've forgotten what——?'

'All right, very funny,' Laurie snapped. 'As it happens, there's nothing I'd like better than to get dressed. All I need is some clothes.'

'And there they are.' He nodded towards a chair. 'Dried—not pressed, I'm afraid, but you're welcome to the use of the iron if it matters to you. But I put them through the machine, so they're pretty clean.'

'My clothes?' Laurie went over to the chair and picked them up unbelievingly. Shirt, shorts, bra and pants. She looked at him.

'Well?' Russ said. 'Don't you want to get dressed after all?'

'Of course I do. But why——?'

Russ grinned broadly. 'Oh, I don't imagine you'll try escaping again, even with clothes on. After seeing your efforts with the sailboard, I've no worries on that score. And I shall make sure you don't have access to paddles for the canoes, or the keys for the motor-boat.'

Laurie gazed at him. 'You were watching me all along this morning. You saw me look at the boats.'

'I did,' he acknowledged cheerfully. 'And very instructive it was, too.' His voice changed. 'As a matter of fact, Laurie, I admire you very much for what you did this morning. You were absolutely determined to get away, and the fact that you'd never touched a sail-board in your life——'

'I have! I've had two lessons.'

'More or less the same thing. Anyway, you knew you'd have problems handling it, but you didn't let that daunt you—you got it put together, rode it out into the lake, and did your best to master it. I appreciate that, Laurie. It took courage.'

'It took desperation! I wanted to get away from here—away from you. And don't take it for granted that I won't try again, the first chance I get.' Laurie stalked out of the kitchen with her clothes, and went upstairs to shower and dress.

Russ was taking the muffins out of the oven when she came down again. They were toasted a golden brown, and he had prepared a platter of bacon and scrambled eggs to go with them. Suddenly ravenous, Laurie sat down and helped herself to a large plateful.

'Well, that's good to see,' he remarked, watching her. 'You do have human appetites after all.'

Laurie stopped eating. 'What do you mean?'

'I mean I was beginning to wonder,' he said smoothly. 'Your response definitely indicates at times that there's a human being lurking somewhere beneath that defensive shell. But the moment you realise what's happening, back you go, like a hermit crab terrified of being recognised. What is it with you, Laurie? What's happened to you to put you off behaving like a mature woman?'

Laurie sat perfectly still. Then she laid down her fork.

'Am I to take it that you're referring to the times when you've tried to force your attentions on me?'

she asked icily, and was disconcerted when Russ gave a yelp of laughter.

'"*Force my attentions*"? Laurie, what a delightfully Victorian way you have of putting things. Forgive me if I'm a little more blunt. The times when I kissed you, yes.' He met her eyes squarely, forcing her to look back at him. 'The times when *you* kissed *me*. Because, make no mistake about it, Laurie, my sweet, you most certainly *did* kiss me. With considerable enthusiasm too, as I recall it.'

Laurie felt a deep flush scorch her neck and cheeks. She wanted to look away, but could not. There was a mesmerising quality in the dark blue eyes that held hers so commandingly. She felt her heartbeat quicken, her pulse race.

'Why do you always back away, Laurie?' he asked quietly. 'What are you afraid of?'

She swallowed. 'Russ, I—I don't want to talk about it. I——'

'You're afraid to talk about it,' he stated. 'You're afraid to face it. But it's there, Laurie. It's there, and it won't go away.'

'What is?' she whispered. 'What's there? I don't know——'

'You do know.' He reached out a strong brown hand and gripped hers. 'You know very well, only you won't admit it. There's something between us, Laurie— something strong, something powerful, something that shouldn't be ignored——'

'You're sounding like a third-rate pulp romance,' Laurie snapped, jerking her hand away. '"Something between us" indeed. In another minute you'll be telling me that "this thing is bigger than both of us". Well, maybe it is. But I tell you this, I'm not afraid to face it, and I know only too well what it is. It's pure, unalloyed dislike—nothing more, nothing less.'

Russ did not move. His eyes flickered slightly, and he asked, 'Why not call it hate? It's what you mean, isn't it?'

'Hate? Why should I call it hate? I've never hated anyone in my life.'

'But you'd like to call it that, all the same. And don't they say that hate is simply the other face of love?' He was watching her steadily. 'Say it, Laurie. One way or the other—say it. And face the truth.'

Laurie stared at him. Then she stood up, knocking her fork to the floor. Her hands clenched themselves into fists, and she physically had to restrain herself from lifting them to strike him.

'I'll say nothing of the sort,' she said in a low, tense voice. 'I won't give you the satisfaction. Because neither is true, Russ. You don't warrant hate. And you certainly don't warrant love!'

For the rest of that day they avoided each other. Or perhaps it would be more true, Laurie thought, to say that she avoided him. Russ didn't seem to make any efforts to be near her, but she was constantly coming across him and having to turn away. He never attempted to follow her, merely lifted one eyebrow and watched her go, then returned to whatever he was doing—reading a book, studying a file, pruning plants in the garden or repairing some fishing tackle.

Eventually, Laurie found a book and took it to a garden-chair to read under the shade of the birch trees. How long she was going to be here, she still didn't know, nor why Russ had chosen this crazy course; but she could not tolerate the boredom of having nothing at all to do. But it was difficult to read; she kept finding herself disturbed by the 'whoosh' of a hummingbird or the flutter of wings in the trees. She laid her book down and watched the birds as they went about their lives, oblivious to the whims of humans. It was something she had loved to do with her parents; her mother in particular had been able to sit still and silent for hours, watching the birds. But there had been so little opportunity once she had moved to Ottawa, and she had never had time to re-discover its joys in Toronto.

'Pretty, aren't they?' Russ observed, passing her with a barrow filled with logs. 'Shame to lose their habitat, don't you think?'

Laurie instantly returned to her book. But it had lost all power to interest her, and after a while she got up and sauntered casually down the path to the little beach.

The canoes and sailboard were still there, but the sail itself had disappeared, and she guessed that Russ didn't trust her not to try to get away again, in spite of her abortive attempt that morning. But it hadn't been that abortive, she thought. She had got the board sailing and might well have escaped if she hadn't been heading for those rocks. She frowned, gazing out across the lake to the spot where Russ had caught her.

What rocks? There were none to be seen—his shouted warning had been nothing but a successful ruse to startle her. She shrugged. It hardly mattered—she would probably have fallen in anyway. But if the sail had been here, she would certainly have tried again.

A small frog hopped into the water ahead of her, and she remembered the heron, stalking along her own beach, its long beak stabbing forwards. What would happen to the heron and the frogs if people like Alec had their way and developed areas like this? Where would they go?

Restlessly, she turned and made her way back to the cottage. And when Russ came in from the wood an hour later she was busy making a salad, while the fresh-baked smell of a pie drifted from the oven. She turned and saw his quizzical expression, and spoke before he could say anything.

'All right. So I might as well make myself useful while I'm here. I enjoy cooking, as it happens—and I don't often have time for it.'

Russ smiled and said nothing. He went upstairs, and she heard him showering. When he came back, he was wearing clean jeans and a fresh shirt. Laurie felt scruffy in the clothes that had been clean enough that morning but were crumpled and dusty now. She put the salad on the table and took the pie from the oven.

'How long are you going to keep me here, Russ?'

He ignored her question. 'I thought we'd go out in the canoe this evening. See what there is to be seen before it gets dark and the mosquitoes come looking for dinner.'

'Russ, I asked you a question.'

'And the answer,' he said, 'depends on you.'

'On when I decide to sleep with you, you mean,' she flashed, and saw his eyes darken at once.

'Whether you sleep with me or not, Laurie, is an entirely separate issue. I'm not asking you to do that——'

'It's not a thing you do ask, is it?' she said bitterly. 'You just take it for granted.'

'Laurie, I could have taken you to bed at any time during the past twenty-four hours——'

'And haven't you tried?'

He sighed. 'No. I haven't tried. The times when I've kissed you have been—well, never mind. You wouldn't believe me anyway.' He stood up abruptly. 'Come on. The sun'll be down in an hour or so. I want to get out on the lake.'

'And doesn't it matter what I want——?'

'Laurie!' His voice was like a whip. 'Quit arguing, and come with me. It's all right—I'm not going to ravish you. I'm not even going to touch you—but I will, if you don't do as I say and *come along*.'

Trembling a little with anger, but afraid to defy him any more, Laurie got up and followed him down to the beach. In silence, he pushed his canoe out into the water, and indicated that she should sit in the bow. She took the paddle he gave her, and they moved slowly out of the little bay and across to the shore.

Paddling along in the failing light, Laurie gazed hopelessly at the shore. So near, yet so far. She thought of letting herself fall overboard, swimming for freedom, but knew that Russ would be after her in a flash. And he had already proved himself stronger than she in the water, just as he was on land. She thought of his hard body catching her against him again under the water, and her spine tingled.

There was a sudden noise onshore, a sound like rapidly thumping footsteps. Laurie caught her breath, and Russ stopped paddling. They both stared towards the shore, waiting for what was approaching the water.

A large beaver erupted from the undergrowth and flung itself at the water with a huge splash. It swam directly towards the canoe, its round head above the water, heavy body half submerged. Then it seemed to see them. It paused briefly, then turned its head neatly downwards and dived, giving the water a resounding smack with its broad, flat tail as it disappeared.

Laurie found that she had been holding her breath. She let it out slowly.

'Well?' Russ said quietly. 'Was that worth seeing?'

'Oh, *yes*,' she replied softly. 'Yes, it was marvellous. It's years since I've seen a beaver, properly.'

'Let's see if we can spot some more,' he said, and they slipped their paddles silently into the calm water and moved on.

By the time they returned to the island they had seen five beavers swimming, and watched two others emerge from the big untidy lodge of sticks that they had built at the water's edge. Laurie marvelled at the size of the trees they had felled. Surely there was no other animal so industrious.

'Not even humans, a lot of the time,' Russ confirmed. 'We're a lazy lot on the whole.'

'I work very hard,' Laurie protested, and he laughed.

'So do I. Present company excepted, of course—isn't it always?'

They pulled the canoe up on the beach and hurried back to the cottage. Darkness was falling, and the mosquitoes would soon be at their thickest and most voracious.

Russ closed the doors securely before switching on the lamp. Then he turned to Laurie. The warm, low light had softened his features. His eyes were very dark.

'Laurie...' he said, and came towards her.

Laurie stood quite still. If he touched her now, she would be lost. During the past two hours all their antagonism had disappeared. She felt at peace with him and with her surroundings. She wanted suddenly, as she had never wanted anything before, to be held close and warm in his arms. She wanted his touch, his kiss.

More than that—she needed them.

Russ moved slowly towards her, stopping with his body almost, but not quite, touching hers. He looked down at her gravely, and she returned his look. There was a long moment of perfect silence. And then he turned away.

'I'm going to my study to do some work,' he said, his voice clipped. He stood with his back to her, remote and unapproachable. 'Make yourself a drink if you like, Laurie. I'll see you in the morning.'

Without looking at her again, he walked up the stairs, and she heard him go into the little room that had been furnished as an office. She heard the door click shut and—unbelievably—a key turn in the lock.

Laurie stood quite still for a very long time. Then, moving stiffly, like a robot, she too went up the stairs and into her room. But, although she went to bed and turned out the light, she did not sleep. She lay for a long time, staring into the darkness until it was darkness no longer, until the cool grey dawn crept through the window and the first bird raised its voice to greet another day.

CHAPTER EIGHT

As THE lake began to brighten from pewter to shimmering blue in the morning sun, Laurie slipped out of bed and went down to the big living-room. It was still and quiet, as if not yet ready to begin the day, and she moved quietly, filling and switching on the coffee-maker, finding bread to make toast, pouring a glass of orange juice.

There was no sound from upstairs as she took her breakfast out to the porch and ate it slowly, gazing out over the lake. At some time during the night she had heard Russ come out of his study and go to his bedroom. She had lain tense, half expecting that he might come in to her—but after a few moments the sound of movement had stopped, and she'd known that he had gone to his own bed. She had imagined him thrusting back that black and gold cover, stretching himself naked under a single sheet, and her own body had grown hot.

During those dark, quiet hours, Laurie had come to face the reality of what had happened to her. She had been struggling against it for weeks, she realised, but it could be denied no longer. And, as the truth had come home to her, she'd felt the tears sting her eyes, and turned her face into her pillow.

Somewhere along the way she had fallen in love with Russ Brandon. And she knew, after his rejection of her last night, that there was no hope.

When had it happened? With that first kiss, when she had felt fire lick through her veins, when his lips had released emotions she hadn't known herself to possess? Or had it been long before that—back as far as that first meeting in her aunt's living-room, when she had looked into eyes of cobalt-blue and felt the earth spin?

Or even earlier, years ago when she was no more than a child, when Russ and his brothers had taken her swimming and fishing? She had idolised him even then; had that feeling persisted, grown into adult love, without her even knowing it?

The questions seemed almost academic. What did it matter when love had begun? The fact was that it was here, burning inside her, impossible to ignore. And utterly hopeless.

Hopeless? Her body cried out in anguish at the thought. Why should it be hopeless? Hadn't Russ kissed her with an urgency that had swept her away in his arms? Hadn't his own body told her that he wanted her?

And hadn't he rejected her last night, just when she had been ready to give herself to him? Hadn't he gone to another room—and locked himself away?

A sound behind her made her turn. Russ was standing in the doorway, looking down at her with sombre eyes. For a moment, they gazed speechlessly at each other; then Laurie turned her head away, not wanting him to see the bright glitter of her tears.

'I made some coffee,' she said, her throat almost too tight to form the words.

'I know.' He took a step towards her, and her heart leapt. Then he stopped. 'Laurie, I'll take you back to your cottage. You were right—I shouldn't have kept you here. I'm sorry.'

Laurie stared up at him.

'You're taking me back? Letting me go? But—why?'

His mouth moved in a wry grin. 'Shouldn't you be asking why I kidnapped you in the first place?'

'No. I know why that was. To make me appreciate the beauty of the lake. To make me change my mind about Alec's plans for development.'

'And has it?' he asked quietly.

Laurie shook her head. 'How could it? Russ, you were wrong——'

His face closed. 'Wrong? Yes, I *was* wrong—to think that I could ever get through to that mercenary little brain of yours. I was wrong to think there might be a heart beating somewhere in that beautiful breast.' Disgust twisted his lean face. 'Do you know, I thought last night—just for a few minutes—that you were softening? I thought that seeing those beavers might just do it. And then, when we came back——'

'What?' she cried. 'What happened? Why did you change your mind?'

'Two things,' he said heavily. 'Your response when I talked about work. You love your job—you love your way of life. You love the material comforts of life, and for those you need money. And when people begin to need money the way you do, they don't stop. They go on and on, wanting more. They'll get it any way they can.'

'Russ!' Even as she recoiled against his words, she knew that they were true—for Alec. That was just how Alec had become in the past few months. His computer business had suddenly taken off, he had become rich, and he had begun to look for other ways of making money—more and more money. Her cottage had come as a golden opportunity to get into a new market—the market of leisure property, one of the fastest growing of the day.

But it wasn't true of her. It had never been true of her.

'Russ, you've got it all wrong,' she protested, controlling her pain in her need to make him understand. 'I never had any intention of letting Alec carry out those plans. I love the lake—I love Uncle Tom's cottage. I want it all to stay the way it is, with the beavers and the loons.'

'Do you really expect me to believe that? When I've twice come upon you discussing those plans, clearly as enthusiastic about them as that fiancé of yours? Just what sort of a fool do you take me for, Laurie?'

Laurie tried to remember what Russ had heard. What had she been saying when he came to the cottage when Alec was there with Morrison? She had a sick feeling that she'd been talking about the development, yes, almost as if she approved of it. But her tone had been sarcastic, her whole attitude negative, hadn't he realised that?

'Russ,' she said, 'there's something you should know. Alec is *not* my fiancé—not any more. I broke the engagement off before I came to the cottage.'

'So why was he there that day? Talking as if he owned the place—or anticipated owning it in the near future?'

'He wouldn't accept it. He——'

'You were wearing his ring,' he reminded her bleakly, and she remembered how Alec had put it on her finger, how Russ had seen it there. 'Have you given it back to him?' She blinked, wanted to say yes, but the ring was still in a box at the cottage, and she could not lie about it. 'So you didn't. You still have it. It doesn't sound as if you were too sure about breaking it off, does it?'

'Russ, it's hard to explain...'

'You're right,' he said. 'And it's hard to understand, too.' He looked down at her for a moment, then suddenly dropped to the step beside her. 'Why, Laurie? Why can't you *see*? What you're planning——'

Laurie's pain began to give way to exasperation. 'No, Russ, why can't *you* see I'm telling you the truth? I've finished with Alec, and I never intended to let these development ideas go through anyway. Besides,' she added, struck by a new thought, 'I doubt if they would be allowed. There must be planning restrictions. There must be conservation laws——'

'There are. But men like Alec Hadlow and that snake Morrison know all the ways of getting round them. I tell you, Laurie, I've been up against that man before. It means a lot of hard fighting, a lot of expense. Going to law is——'

'An ideal opportunity for people like you to make money,' she interrupted heatedly. 'Don't they always say that the only people to benefit from lawsuits are the lawyers? Is that how you make your money, Russ, fighting for people's rights and making them poor in the process? Did you make a fortune out of that other lake you told me about—the one Morrison wanted to develop? Do you mean to make a fortune out of this one too?'

There was shock on his face as he stared at her, then a bitterness she had never seen before. He shook his head slowly, and Laurie felt a sudden chill, as if she had gone too far, said too much.

'Well, I guess you might be expected to believe that,' he said quietly. 'Corruption sees corruption wherever it looks. And you've been corrupted. Maybe it wasn't your fault. I wouldn't know. But I want you to know this, Laurie. I didn't make a penny out of that fight. I never presented a bill. I was glad to save the lake, and glad to see Morrison go down.

'Yes, go down,' he repeated, his eyes like stones. 'He went to gaol over that little episode—false documents that he tried to present—and I didn't expect to see him around these parts again for a long while. But since he's here, I may as well tell you that I'll fight him again, every inch of the way, him and your precious Alec Hadlow. And I'll fight them if it takes every penny *I* have, because that's why I'm a lawyer. To right wrongs.'

His glance seared her frozen face. 'I take money for what I do because I have to make a living,' he told her quietly. 'But I'm employed by people who can afford my terms. Other cases I take on because I believe in them—and then I charge only what my clients can afford. Not,' he added, turning away, 'that it's really any of your business.'

Laurie was silent. She felt a warm shame creeping over her body. She had completely misread him, she thought miserably, and she deserved his scorn. But hadn't he misread her too?

She waited for a moment, then said softly, 'You said there were two reasons why you would take me back, Russ. What was the other?'

He looked at her, then away at the lake. His expression was remote, but she was beginning to know that this concealed intense emotion. She waited with sudden fear.

'The way you looked at me when we came in last night,' he revealed slowly. 'You wanted me to make love to you, Laurie. And I—God help me—I wanted to make love to you.'

Laurie stopped breathing.

'Then . . . why didn't you?' she asked in a whisper.

'Why?' He turned his head again, and she shrank back from the expression in his eyes, the torment, the fury, the pain. 'If only I could—if only I could make love to you, just once, and get this—this fever out of my system. Oh, I would—don't imagine I wouldn't. But it wouldn't be like that. If I made love to you once, Laurie, just once, I'd be bound to you for the rest of my life. You'd be my woman—do you understand? I'd never be able to leave you—never. And the thought of being committed to a woman whose main interest is money; well, it's a thought I simply can't—*won't*—tolerate.' He stood up abruptly and swung away from her. 'Finish your coffee, Laurie. I'm taking you back to your cottage—now.'

He went into the house and emerged a few minutes later with the box of groceries that Laurie had bought in the village—it seemed like a lifetime ago. With neither a word nor a glance, he set off down the path to the beach, and Laurie, miserable and helpless, followed him.

She watched as he put the groceries into her canoe and then fastened the craft to his motor-boat. As he motioned to her to get into the boat, she touched his arm, looking up into his face.

'Russ——'

'Don't,' he said harshly. 'Just—don't. It won't help, Laurie.'

'But, Russ—you must believe me——'

'I don't want to hear.' His voice had a note of finality, and she knew he would not listen. Numb with misery, she dropped her hand and turned to step into the boat.

Russ said no more until they were at her own small beach. He brought the motor-boat alongside the jetty, where her own boat—Tom's—bobbed gently in the water, and he carried the box of groceries ashore. He unfastened the painter of the canoe, and pulled the craft up on the beach. Only then did he permit himself a brief glance at her.

'That's it, then, Laurie. No doubt I'll see you when your three months are up, and you come to the office to sign the deeds to the cottage. Though I think it would probably be better if you saw one of my colleagues. I'll arrange that.'

'Russ——' Laurie began desperately, but again he cut her short.

'I'll say goodbye, then.' And there was no doubt that he meant *goodbye*, in its real sense. If Russ had his way, they would never set eyes on each other again.

It couldn't happen. It mustn't happen.

'Russ—*please*.' Her hands were on his arms, her fingers tight on the hard muscles. 'Russ, you can't go like this. There's too much to say; we need to talk——'

'There's been enough said already.' His voice dropped to no more than a breath. 'Too much.'

'No. *No*. We haven't begun to talk properly. We've just made assumptions, accusations. You're wrong about me, Russ. You must listen. You must give me a chance—just one chance.'

'And haven't I done that already?' he asked bitterly, but she shook her head.

'Not properly, no. You've never let me *talk*. We've never given each other time.'

He hesitated. His eyes came reluctantly to meet hers, and her heart leapt. There was a chance—there must be a chance.

'Please,' she said in a low, intense tone, 'please, Russ, come into the cottage. Or stay out here if you like. But please listen to me—just for a while.' There was doubt in his expression, but she could see that he was wavering. If only he would agree. If only he would let her explain—if only he would believe her...

Russ opened his mouth to speak. But his first words were lost in the sound of a car coming down the track. And, as they turned to see who it was, Laurie felt her heart sink.

The big car turned in under the birches, and stopped. She heard Russ mutter something under his breath. And then Alec got out, waving cheerfully, and Laurie saw that Sam Morrison was with him.

'Hi!' Alec called. 'I'm glad you're around—we thought you'd still be snoring at this hour! I've brought the plans for you to see—and some figures.' He was coming down through the grove, beaming expansively. 'These are going to interest you, Laurie,' he said. 'The kind of profit we're going to make here will put computers right back in the shade.'

Laurie stared at him. Then she turned to look at Russ.

He ignored the hand she held out to him. As if he could bear to look at her no longer, he turned away.

He strode to his boat as if the very sand under his feet were contaminated, and jerked the painter from its post.

'Russ!' Laurie cried, running along the jetty. But she might as well not have existed. Russ started the engine, reversed the boat away from the jetty, then swung it round in an arc. He was gone at full throttle, with a roar that brought several ducks flying from the rocks in panic.

Laurie stood on the jetty, staring after him. And, when he had disappeared around the end of the little bay, she turned to walk slowly back to the beach to face the man who had come in his big, shining car and destroyed the peace of her paradise.

The man she had once thought she could spend the rest of her life with.

Slowly, the days shortened. The leaves on the trees began to lose their fresh green and turn slowly to the rich colours of autumn: tawny brown, honey-gold, burning red. The woods that came down to the shores of the lake were like a shawl of rich, glowing tapestries, thrown carelessly around the shoulders of the hills. The sun burnished them to a deeper glow and, against all the flaming colour, the sky looked a more tender, delicate blue.

It was almost time for Laurie to go back to Ottawa, to go to Russ's office and sign the final documents that would grant her possession of the cottage. And then? What was she to do then?

Return to Toronto, she supposed. Go back to her job in the fashion house, her smart little flat, her friends who enjoyed city life and would never dream of spending three months in a lonely lakeside cottage.

Who no doubt thought she was mad to do so. If they thought of her at all. If they hadn't forgotten all about her.

She took her canoe out on the lake, paddling slowly along on the cool, still water, her eyes seeing everything very brightly, very clearly, as if she had been given a sharper vision. She looked from side to side, noting the changes on the shoreline she had come to know so well.

The autumn leaves floated on the water like scraps of brilliant silk. The osprey drifted high overhead, its keen eyes searching for fish beneath the surface of the water. And then Laurie heard a rapid whistling, a beating of huge wings, and looked up.

The loons were approaching fast down the lake. There was 'her' loon, the big black diver that had been almost a companion, swimming near enough for her to see the stripes on his neck, crying his lonely lament as dusk fell. And now he was joined by other loons, from other parts of the lake and from neighbouring lakes. From lakes much further north too, the birds waiting for each other until they could migrate together. They filled the sky, like a massed black cloud as they began their long flight down to Florida or the Carolina seaboard for the winter.

Laurie sat quite still, watching as the birds flew steadily overhead. It was as if something had come to an end—as if the loons, by leaving the lake, had taken with them something that was hers. And she knew that it was time for her to go too.

Whatever she had come here to find—peace, tranquillity, a haven?—had slipped through her fingers. And the lake was a cold, lonely place for her now.

*   *   *

Laurie's heart was beating fast when she went to Russ's office to sign the documents that would make the cottage hers. The thought of seeing him after so many weeks, and especially after their last parting, was almost enough to make her want to turn tail and run. How would he react to seeing her again? How would he look at her, speak to her? She remembered the words he had said—she had remembered them every day, almost every hour since, as if they were branded in her mind: 'If I made love to you once, Laurie, just once, I'd be bound to you for the rest of my life . . . I'd never be able to leave you—never.'

Had he really said those words, or had she imagined them? Had he meant them?

For the hundredth time, Laurie tried to analyse what he had meant. He wasn't in love with her—he had made that very clear. Yet there was some chemistry between them, some powerful attraction that he had felt, that told him that once that final bond had been forged there would be no escape for either of them. And the fact that she loved him—as she knew she did, as every sleepless night told her she did— would not be enough to save them from disaster.

It needed more than one love, she thought sadly. And she knew that life with Russ, knowing that she did not have his love, would be a torment.

But then, so was life without him.

The lift whisked her up to the high floor where his office was situated, and she stepped out and walked along the thickly carpeted corridor to the door. She felt sick with apprehension. In a few moments that door would open, she would walk inside, it would close again behind her, and she would be with Russ again. Face to face. Able to touch him—if she dared.

Able to look at him—but would she be able to hide what she felt? Would she be able to keep her heart from her eyes?

She reached the door and stopped. She raised a trembling hand to knock. The door opened. And Laurie looked up into a lean, tanned face, into eyes of a blue as dark as cobalt. She looked at hair the deep auburn of the leaves that had floated on the lake, at a mouth that widened into a smile that revealed white, even teeth.

'Good morning, Laurie.' The deep voice was remote, uncompromisingly hard. She could have been any visitor. Any unwelcome visitor, she amended. And she knew that he had neither forgotten nor forgiven that last day at the lake. But then, how could she have expected it?

'Russ...' She followed him into the office. The coffee-maker bubbled quietly on the side-table, and he gestured towards it, but she shook her head, numb with misery. She saw the documents on the table, ready for her signature. Clearly, he wanted the whole business over and done with just as much as she did.

'And how do you like being back in the city?' he asked formally when they had finished. 'I imagine you find it quite a relief, being back among the shops, civilisation and all that.'

'No more than you do, no doubt,' she replied evenly, letting her eyes move over his well-cut business suit. 'You seem able to move between the two worlds happily enough—why not allow others to do the same?'

He inclined his head, but the cobalt eyes were still unsmiling. 'And Hadlow—I suppose he's eager to get on with his schemes for the development? When will you be submitting your plans?'

'There won't be any plans. I told you, the engagement's off—it's been off for a long time, since before I first went to the lake. Alec came to try to persuade me again, but I was always against it.' She lifted her eyes to his face. 'You never believed me, Russ, and I don't suppose you believe me now, but you'll see that it's true.'

She remembered the scene after Russ had left them that day. Alec and Morrison, standing on the beach, glossy and complacent, smiling as if they had no doubt that she would agree to their plans. Behaving as if she had no say at all in what happened to her own property.

'Well,' Alec had said, looking out across the peaceful water, 'what got into him?' He looked sharply at Laurie. 'There's nothing going on between him and you, is there?'

Laurie turned and stared at him blankly.

'No,' she replied, and misery flooded through her at the word, 'no, there's not. Though it would be nothing to do with you if there were. Our engagement's broken, Alec, remember?'

'Oh, Laurie, you're not still——'

'Not still what? I've been trying to make you understand this for weeks—months.' She stared at him, realising just what he had done, realising that there could now be no hope of her ever convincing Russ of the truth.

'Look, all I've ever done is act in your best interests——'

'*My* best interests? How can turning my cottage into a—a second-class Disneyland be in *my* best interests?

And how dare you come here with your horrible plans, after all I said last time?' Her voice was trembling. 'How dare you even set foot on my land?' She took a step towards him, and Alec, startled by her sudden fury, backed away.

'Get out,' she spat, and felt a surge of emotion so violent that it frightened her. 'Get out of here—away from my home—and take your plans with you. And don't ever—*ever* come back! Do you hear me? I never want to see you or hear from you again—and this time you'll take your ring with you too. I never liked it anyway.'

She stalked past him and up to the house, ignoring Sam Morrison, who was standing uncertainly by the porch steps. She walked into her bedroom, took the ring out of the drawer where she had put it, and marched outside again.

Alec was standing with Morrison, looking uneasy but already trying, she could see, to bluff his way out of his embarrassment. Laurie went down the steps, and thrust the box into his hand.

'There you are. All present and correct. Take it and go away. And never, never come back—either of you.' She gave them both one last searing glance, then went back into the cottage and shut the door firmly, locking it behind her. Without waiting to see what they would do, she went up the steps and back into her bedroom.

It had seemed a long time before she heard the car go at last, and until then she sat dry-eyed on the bed, tense and waiting.

But with the sound of the engine fading into the distance she had flung herself down on the pillows and burst into a tempest of weeping. And knew that she was weeping not for Alec and all she had rejected,

but for what he had done to her. For the damage he
had caused in her life.

And the pain was still there, she thought now,
looking at Russ in his business suit, so at home in his
city office yet bringing a tang of the outdoors, as if
he never completely left the wildness of the lake
behind. If only she could tell him all that had happened, convince him that she had never gone along
with Alec's plans. If only there was a chance that he
would believe her.

'There won't be any plans,' she repeated, her voice
dry. 'Alec and I are not getting married. And even if
we had——'

'You'll be selling, then, I take it?' he said as if she
hadn't mentioned Alec. 'Not a good time now, with
winter coming on, but you should get a reasonable
price...'

It was exactly what her uncle had said, and she remembered his exasperation when she had refuted his
words. 'Sell? I'm not going to sell—it's mine; I'm
keeping it.'

And Russ echoed John Marchant's words again
when he said, 'Keeping it? What for? What do you
want with a lake cottage—especially one so far from
Toronto? You'd never be able to use it.' She was back
again in her uncle's living-room, hearing the voice that
had dominated her childhood. 'You're just being
foolish and sentimental, Laurie. If you want a cottage
that badly, buy one a bit nearer Toronto. I've got a
friend in real estate; he'll give you some advice——'

'I don't want advice!' Laurie had cried then, and
seen the shock registering on her aunt's face, the fury
on her uncle's. But she wasn't afraid of them any
more. She wasn't afraid of upsetting her aunt, of the

disappointment she would see in the timid eyes that had used their own power over her. She wasn't afraid of her uncle's temper, his overwhelming desire to rule her. She was her own person at last and she could speak for herself. She caught her breath, realising that they had no power over her now, and when she'd spoken again her voice had been calm. As it was now, when she spoke to Russ and repeated the words she had said then.

'I need that cottage,' she told him. 'It's important to me. It stands for something in my life. It's a—a sort of focus.'

'A focus?' Russ asked quietly.

'Yes. My mother and father built that cottage with their own hands. I spent eight years of my childhood there. How could I sell it to a stranger now?'

'You didn't go there for seventeen years,' he reminded her.

'Because they never let me. They kept the letters your mother wrote to me, they kept Uncle Tom's letters, and let me think no one was interested in me. Oh, I know why they did it; they genuinely believed it was best, that it would unsettle me to go backwards and forwards between two lives. At least, Aunt Ella did. Uncle John . . . I don't know. He wanted to bring me up in his way, and he never stopped to wonder if it was right. He never does; he's the sort of man who believes he *is* right. Always.'

She looked up and caught the flicker of an expression on Russ's face, but as she paused he merely lifted his brows, and after a moment she continued. She wasn't sure why she was telling him all this— hadn't he already shown that any relationship between them was doomed?—but she didn't want to leave this office without at least trying to put the record straight.

'They took my childhood away from me,' she went on slowly. 'My mother—you remember her, Russ. She was pretty, popular, good at everything; Aunt Ella was always left in the shade. They grew up, and Mum married the most popular boy in town, and Aunt Ella married my uncle, who was a lot older, a successful banker. She had everything then, materially—but she never had what my mother had. She never had any children.'

'There were other things she didn't have,' Russ said, and Laurie nodded.

'I know. She didn't have the fun my mother had. There was never the laughter in my aunt's house, never the excitement, the chaos, the friends dropping in, the sudden outings, the games, the sing-songs...' Her voice faded, remembering the brightness of those days so long ago. 'There was never the love,' she concluded, and fell silent.

'Even though in the end she *did* have everything?' Russ said at last. 'After the accident? She had you then, a child to bring up as her own. And she had her life—which your parents didn't have any more.'

Laurie was silent, remembering how Aunt Ella had expressed it. Her longing for a child had been appeased at last. 'An answer to a prayer', she had said. Her own sister's death, the answer to a prayer... But it hadn't been like that—not really. Surely it hadn't been like that...

'You ought to have let me go back,' she had said to them. 'You shouldn't have cut me off.'

And then her uncle had thrown down his cigar and risen to his feet, his face dark and angry.

'Now see here, Laurie, I'm getting tired of this. You seem to think you can duck in and out of here whenever you feel like it, telling us what we should and shouldn't have done. We gave you a home, right? It was that or an orphanage; which do you prefer? We gave you a proper education, which you weren't getting out at that lake, even if your mother was a qualified teacher. We taught you what life was really all about—not a permanent holiday but a serious business, where everyone pulls their own weight. If we hadn't done that, would you be where you are now? Would you have a good job, a classy flat, the chance to marry well? I doubt it, Laurie. I doubt it very much indeed.' He'd turned to his wife. 'I'm going out now, Ella. I've got business to see to. Dinner at seven, prompt, please. There's no reason why this ungrateful chit should disrupt our life any more than she has already.'

There had been a silence then. Laurie saw her aunt's fingers plucking at the hem of her dress, and felt suddenly sorry for the older woman, who seemed to have so much—a successful husband, a beautiful home, a circle of society friends—and yet had nothing. It was all a façade. She saw the emptiness and shuddered, realising how nearly it had happened to her.

'My parents weren't feckless or irresponsible,' she protested at last. 'They just had different values.'

'I know,' Ella said quietly. 'But none of us can go against our own natures. I did my best for you, Laurie, as I saw it. I know now that I should have let you go back.' She lifted her eyes, and Laurie saw that they were full of tears. 'I'm very sorry.'

The simple apology touched Laurie's heart, and she went swiftly to her aunt's side and put her arms around her.

It was the first real embrace she ever remembered them sharing.

Looking at Russ now, she wondered if he could understand any of this. She had to tell him, but was she talking to a closed mind, or was something of her emotion getting through to him? Was she striking any kind of chord? She could not tell. The lean face was as unreadable as ever, the dark eyes veiled.

'The cottage is all I have left of that life,' she explained. 'I have to keep it.'

He nodded. Then he drew the documents across the desk towards him. He slipped them into a large envelope, passed them back to her, and stood up. 'Well, it's yours now,' he said, his voice coolly unemotional. 'And I hope you find what you need there. No doubt we'll run into each other from time to time. And now, if you'll excuse me... I believe I have another appointment due.'

Laurie stared at him blankly. She felt as if she had been slapped in the face. She had opened her heart to him—and been rebuffed. Oh, he had listened—at least, he hadn't interrupted. But had her words meant anything to him at all?

As she walked away towards the lift, without any idea as to how she had said goodbye or got out of his office, she felt a numb misery settle over her body, weighing it down like a thick grey blanket. And she knew that, whatever had been growing between her and Russ Brandon, it had died. Somewhere, in all the things that had happened between them, it had died. It just hadn't been strong enough to live.

CHAPTER NINE

It was mid-December before Laurie could go back to the cottage again. After three months' leave, giving in her notice at work had been a difficult thing to do, and she had felt compelled to offer as much help as possible in recruiting a replacement from the staff and helping her to settle into the job. At the same time, she had had to make arrangements to put her own apartment on the market, and decide which of her furniture should be stored and which taken to the cottage. And she had no idea what she was going to do to earn her living once she was there. That was something she'd have to think about later. .

Her friends had, naturally, all thought she was crazy. And Uncle John and Aunt Ella had been totally unable to understand.

'You've taken leave of your senses!' John had declared when they had driven to Toronto to try to talk her out of her plans. 'Laurie, you need help. Treatment. Look, I've a friend who's a psychiatrist; why don't you let me——?'

'No, Uncle John. Thank you, but I'm perfectly sane and perfectly well aware of what I'm doing. The flat will fetch a good price, which I can invest, so I won't be bankrupt. And, after all, you did want me to sell one of my properties,' she added wickedly.

'But not *this* one! Oh——' he gave her an exasperated look '——I can see you're not going to take any notice. We may as well go. Come on, Ella.'

'But we've only just arrived!' his wife protested. 'I haven't had any time to chat with Laurie yet. Can't we——?' But John was already halfway out of the door, and she stopped and gave Laurie a helpless glance.

'It's all right, Aunt Ella,' Laurie said, hugging her warmly. 'I understand. And don't worry about me—I'll be all right. Really.' She hesitated, then explained, 'I have to do this. I feel as if I've begun to discover myself—the real Laurie. After all these years!' She laughed a little. 'I thought I was a "city person"—a career girl, just as you and Uncle John wanted me to be. Someone who knew exactly where she was going and was halfway there. But where was "there"? And what would I have found? I'll tell you, Aunt Ella—nowhere and nothing. It was all a mirage.'

Her aunt had looked at her anxiously—looking, Laurie thought, for signs of the madness her uncle had diagnosed.

'Laurie——'

'Don't worry about it,' Laurie said again. 'Let's just say I was squeezed into the wrong mould, and now I've found my way out. It wasn't your fault, but, as you say, we can't go against our own natures. I've simply reverted to the person I really am. And I have to go back—back to the lake, to the cottage.' A loud hooting from the street told them that John Marchant was growing impatient. Laurie went to the window and stared out, speaking almost as if to herself. 'It hasn't finished with me yet. There's still something I have to find there . . .'

The hunger in her heart told her just what that was. And, although she had little hope of ever finding it now, she still had to try.

And now, driving the last few miles towards the cottage, she felt as if she was coming home.

But it was very different from her last visit. Then, as she'd driven away, the woods had been ablaze with colour; now they were stark in black and white, their leafless branches silhouetted against deep white snow. A stillness lay over the landscape, a silence that was almost tangible. No birds sang, no animals rustled in the undergrowth. And as she parked the car at the entrance to the track, knowing that it would be impossible to drive down it, Laurie felt a shiver. Was she really crazy, coming here like this? Wouldn't it have been better, after all, to wait until spring?

No. Whatever was compelling her to come to the lake, it wanted her now. And she wanted to be there, snug in the small wooden cabin with a log fire, looking out at the frozen lake.

Laurie took her rucksack from the car. It was packed with her immediate needs—perishable foods, some clothes. The rest were packed in bags, ready to be pushed easily into the rucksack when she brought it back, empty, tomorrow. In this way, she could transport all she needed from the car. And there were clothes and stored foods at the cottage.

She unstrapped her skis from the roof-rack and fastened them to her feet. Swinging the rucksack on to her back, she set off, poling along the track, feeling the crispness of the snow beneath the long, narrow skis, delighting in the silence and the beauty of the winter landscape.

It did not take long to ski along the track. And then she was making the last turn, coming to a stop under the birch trees, gazing at the cottage beneath its thick white mantle, with snow piled around it, and at the thick opaque ice of the lake beyond.

It was utterly still. Not a leaf moved. There was not even the faintest tremble of a breeze.

Laurie took off her skis and went up the steps of the porch. She opened the door and stepped inside.

Much later, with the fire lit, the smell of hot soup bubbling in the air and a warm glow cast over the room by the lamps, Laurie felt a little better. She curled up on the sofa, sipping at the mug of soup, and wondered just what she had expected to find. The fire already lit, a meal in the oven and a warm welcome from someone who loved her?

She smiled wryly. For a time, she must have been back in her childhood, coming home with her father after a happy afternoon's skating to find her mother busy preparing supper, a kettle boiling for tea and a fire burning in the hearth. But that time had gone for ever. She wasn't a child now; she was an adult, and any fires had to be lit by herself, any meals prepared and cooked by her own hands.

That was the message of the lake and the cottage. That she must learn to be responsible for herself, not to rely on others. And that was why she had come back. The message had been partially delivered during that summer, but there was still something she needed to learn. That final step towards total self-reliance.

Well, winter here amid the snow and ice should do any teaching still necessary, she thought and, noticing that it was growing dark, went outside for some logs from the stack.

Through the pencilled branches of the trees she could see far out over the lake. The far shore, usually hidden, was clearly visible. And as she stood there, gazing at the heavy sky and wondering if it meant more snow, she noticed that she could also see an island. Russ's island.

And, as she watched, she saw a light. As if someone on that island, in that cottage where he had kept her against her will—but had it really been against her will?—had just decided that it was dark enough to turn on a light.

As if someone was there. Signalling to her.

Laurie picked up her basket of logs, and turned abruptly to go inside. It couldn't be Russ. Not at this time of year. Not out there on the island. It must have been something else. A light on the far shore. A star low in the sky. Or maybe just her imagination.

Laurie locked the door behind her, and drew the curtains. She read for the rest of the evening, then went to bed and snuggled down under her patchwork quilt. But of what she read, she remembered nothing. And, although she lay very still, she could not sleep.

Her head was filled with images of one man. Russ Brandon. Tall, lean, tanned. Smiling, sombre, watchful, lazy. Holding her close in the water, his lips on hers, his legs tangling with hers as they floated together. Holding her close beside a fire, with a blanket half wrapped around her, his fingers touching her skin, trailing fire down her breast. Telling her that if he once made love to her, just once, he would be bound to her for life—even though he clearly did not love her. Leaving her, because he would not listen to her.

Taking her heart with him.

Oh, Russ, Russ, she thought in agony, why wouldn't you listen, why wouldn't you stay, why wouldn't you love me? Because I love you—more than I can say. I love you with every particle of my being. And that's why I've come back here—to be near you. Because I can't bear to be away.

And that, she thought, burying her head in her pillow, simply proves that everyone else is right. I *am* crazy. I ought to be going away, far away, trying to get over this man who despises me. Not coming back here to torture myself.

It did not snow that night. When Laurie woke next morning, it was to a day of clear skies and sparkling frost. The trees glittered with ice, the sun striking them with a thousand rainbows, and the snow was covered with diamanté crystals, like shards of fragile glass. The lake was as smooth as a mirror, and Laurie could hardly wait to eat breakfast before she went outside on the jetty, warmly dressed in a red lined sweater and black ski-pants, fastening on her skates.

It was a long time since she had skated, but after a few faltering steps she realised that it was a skill that never got lost, and she struck out across the ice, feeling her skates bite into the surface of the thick ice. The sun touched her cheeks with cool fingers and she could feel the sting of cold air, but her limbs tingled with the delight of exercise on a crisp, cold morning.

The lake was quite empty. Nothing moved; it was as if she were the only living creature for miles. She passed Russ's island, unable to resist glancing at it as she went by, but there was no sign of life. She must have imagined that light. Or maybe it had been a star after all.

It was a strange feeling, to be out there on the lake where she had paddled in her canoe or driven her small motor-boat. She remembered the day she had tried to escape from the island on Russ's sailboard, and how easily he had caught her. Well, he would have difficulty in catching her now. Not that I'd be trying to escape now, she thought ruefully, and sighed.

She rounded the end of the island, intending to return to the cottage by way of the bay where they had seen the beavers. And, as she came within sight of Russ's harbour, a figure glided out from under the trees and headed straight towards her.

There was no doubt about who it was. There was never any doubt about who it was.

'Russ...' she whispered, and wanted to turn, and run, to skate as fast as possible in the opposite direction. Who had just said she wouldn't be trying to escape? But her body would not obey her panic-stricken commands. Her legs would not perform the necessary turns. She kept going, her eyes fixed on that skimming figure, her heart thumping raggedly in her breast.

This was what she had come for, she thought with a sense of—what? Doom? Destiny? It wasn't the cottage at all. It was this—this man, whose lean face and dark, bright eyes had haunted her dreams, this man who had held her in his arms and brought a tingle to her limbs, who had kissed her and set her whole body burning and trembling—this was what she had come for. This confrontation, which could not be avoided, which had been ordained for years.

The two skaters came closer. She could see his eyes now, fastened on her with a kind of hunger. She could see the set of his jaw, sense the tension in his body, almost hear the beating of his heart.

They stopped no more than a foot apart.

'Laurie,' Russ said slowly, and she raised her eyes to meet his. 'Laurie...'

She looked at him dumbly, not knowing what to say. He was looking at her with a strange dark pain in his eyes. He half reached out, then drew back his hand. She wanted to move, to touch him, and could not.

'So you've come back,' he stated, and there was a sudden harshness in his voice, as if the words hurt him. 'But, of course, you'll be offering winter sports as well, won't you?'

Laurie blinked. It was so long now since she had seen Alec, even thought about him, that she had forgotten all about the proposed development. But Russ clearly hadn't. She shook her head.

'Russ, there's going to be no development. I told you that before. And Alec and I are not engaged. Look——' she pulled off her glove, showed him her bare hand '—I really did give him back his ring. And I told him I never wanted to see him again. Can't you believe me?'

He stared at her. 'But the cottage is yours now——'

'Yes. Mine. And it's going to stay mine—and just the way it always has been.' She had courage now to lay her hand on his arm. 'Russ, I've never wanted anything else. Alec was a mistake. I'd begun to realise it that day when you came to my uncle's house in Ottawa, the day before Canada Day. Please—if you believe nothing else I tell you, believe that.'

He looked deep into her eyes, and she saw something change in the sapphire depths. The tension in his body slackened a little, but she could see that there was still doubt in his mind. She cast about for a way to convince him of the truth. How could she make him trust her, believe in her?

'That day I came to your cottage,' she said quietly, 'I knew it then. I knew it the evening I first arrived and heard the loon. It was as if it had a message for me—a message from my uncle Tom. And I heard it, even though I didn't fully understand it then. But I grew to understand it from that first morning when I went swimming.' She kept her eyes on his, knowing that her colour was rising as they both remembered that encounter, with Russ looking down from his canoe at Laurie as she'd swum naked in the clear waters.

'I understood more and more as I watched the hummingbirds and the herons and the osprey. When we went to look for beavers, I knew that none of this must ever be changed—but I knew more than that.' Her eyes were clear, direct. 'And that day of the thunderstorm, paddling my canoe along the lake, taking shelter on your island—it wasn't what you thought, Russ. I'd already broken my engagement to Alec.'

'Why didn't you tell me?' he asked in a low voice.

'I was afraid to,' she replied simply, and knew she didn't have to explain why.

The beginning of a smile touched his lips, and she drew on all her courage.

'Russ,' she said, 'why don't you take me back to your island? I'd love a cup of hot coffee—and I think we ought to talk.'

'Aren't you afraid I'll kidnap you again?' he asked with a wry lift of his eyebrows, and Laurie laughed.

'Difficult, with the lake frozen. I think I'm safe enough this time.' But do I want to be safe? she wondered as they turned to skate back to the island. Do

I want to get away? And, while she knew that the answer was surely no, she knew also that this time Russ would not try to keep her there. Whatever feeling he had had for her, it had disappeared. He was now no more than he had been years ago—the boy next door. A friend.

Was there really any use in going back with him? Wouldn't it hurt all the more when they parted once again and she knew for certain that her love was hopeless? Wouldn't it be better to draw back now, to protect herself from more pain?

Yes, she acknowledged as she skimmed along in his wake, it undoubtedly would. But the temptation to spend one more hour in his company, to let herself look at him, listen to him, simply be with him, just for this last time, was too great. They might never meet again; she might spend a lifetime yearning for him. But she could not let him go without at least a silent goodbye.

Russ skated straight into the harbour, and sat on a rock to take off his skates. Laurie hesitated, re- alising that she had no shoes to put on, and he glanced up and realised her problem.

'You can't walk up the path barefoot this morning; you'll get frost-bite.'

'Perhaps you've got some boots or something I could use, up at the cottage?' she suggested. 'I could wait here.'

'No need. I'll carry you.'

'You can't—not all that way. I'm too heavy.'

'Rubbish. I've carried heavier feathers.' He stood up. 'Come on—take your skates off; I don't intend to get cut to ribbons. Well, move, Laurie! We'll soon get cold standing about.'

Obediently, she sat down to unlace her skates. Russ moved to the rock behind her, bent and swung her into his arms. He held her for a moment, their faces close, and looked into her eyes.

Laurie felt a spasm of excitement. His lips were only inches away from hers, his breath was warm on her cold cheek. His arms held her firmly, curving round her body so that she was snuggled against his chest, and she could feel his hands splayed, one around her shoulder, the other across her bottom. Automatically, she slipped her own arms around his neck, and her fingers strayed into his hair. Her lips parted.

Russ's mouth tightened and his eyes became opaque, looking past her. He turned and began to climb the snowy path to the cottage. Laurie closed her eyes against the pain of his silent rejection, and tried to imagine that he was carrying her with love, with tenderness, that they were truly, mutually in love, and that he was taking her with swift, long strides to the place where they could be alone to celebrate that love. It was a fantasy, she knew, and could never be anything else—but, just for these few moments, could she not indulge in that fantasy?

All too soon, they were at the cottage. Russ mounted the steps, opened the door, and set her down inside. Laurie opened her eyes reluctantly, knowing that the dream must end, and looked around.

The cottage was as she had seen it in the summer, but the big, comfortable room was now warmed by a wood-stove and there was a log fire in the hearth, ready to be lit. The smell of coffee and hot bread filled the air, and she saw two fresh-baked loaves standing on the kitchen bench. Walking across to touch them, she found that they were still warm.

'Don't tell me you're a baker, among all your other skills?'

'Why not? Bread's simple to make, and I like my fresh rolls for breakfast. Everyone should be able to cook, anyway.' Russ went to the coffee-maker. 'I take it you'd like some?'

'Mmm, please.' Laurie wandered over to the sofa with its view over the icy expanse of the lake. Through the tracery of branches she could see her own bay, and knew that her cottage stood hidden in its own grove. But the light would be visible at night, she thought, and wondered if Russ had seen it last night, as she had seen his.

He would have known that she was here. Had he come out this morning on purpose to meet her? Her heart skipped at the thought, but she dismissed it im-. mediately. Russ had not made any effort to avoid her this morning, it was true; but she was equally sure he would have made no effort to meet her.

'Coffee,' Russ's deep voice said in her ear, and she turned to find him close behind her. She looked into his eyes and caught her breath. Oh, Russ, *Russ* ... But again he drew that veil over his expression, and she took the mug he held out and sat down on the couch.

'I'll light the fire,' he said, going down on his knees. 'The stove keeps the place cosy enough, but I like the flames too. How about you, Laurie—do you enjoy flames?'

His voice was as soft and deep as the snow outside. Laurie could only whisper her reply. 'Yes, I do.' The flames you light in my heart, she thought. But she could not say so. She gazed at him as he knelt there, his back to her, gently coaxing the fire into life. And she had to clench her hands together to prevent herself reaching out, touching that crisp tawny hair, laying her hands on those broad shoulders.

He seemed to stay there for longer than necessary, watching until the fire was well alight. At last he turned and looked straight at her. 'Well, Laurie. You said we should talk. So what do you have to tell me?'

She swallowed. It wasn't easy, starting like this. And his face told her nothing. 'What do you want to know?'

He shrugged. 'What is there to know? You've broken your engagement, which seems to indicate that you do have some sense. You say you don't intend to let the cottage and land be developed. What else?'

She bit her lip. 'Russ, you're not helping——'

'Should I?'

'Please——'

'Please what?' he asked quietly. 'Laurie, I don't know what's in your mind. How can I know? I've never been able to read you—or at least I think I do, and then something happens that turns all my ideas on their heads. You told me before that you didn't want to develop—and the words were hardly out of your mouth when Hadlow arrived waving plans. You told me you'd broken the engagement, yet you still had his ring. Now you come here in the middle of winter, and I'm expected to know why. And I don't.'

She looked at him, making no attempt now to hide the emotion in her eyes and voice. 'Can't you guess?'

'I could,' he said, 'but I'm scared I'd be wrong again.'

With a swift movement, Laurie slipped from the sofa to the rug where he still sat, his long legs folded beneath him. She risked rejection again, she knew—

but one of them had to take that risk. And if she went away from here today, still without his love, knowing she could never have it—well, she'd be no worse off than she'd been when she came.

'Russ,' she said intensely, 'guess. Please. Or, if you won't, listen to me just this once more. I came to the lake because I love it here. It talks to me. It tells me who I am—and I needed to be told that. I came because when I went back to Toronto everything felt wrong. My job, my apartment, the people I knew— nothing seemed to fit any more. And I knew that it was only here that I could find my true self again.'

'So you decided to take a holiday. Well——'

'*No*. Not a holiday, Russ. I've given it all up, that other life. I've left my job, sold my apartment, stored my furniture. I'm going to stay here for the rest of the winter. Then I'll decide what to do; I'll need to work at something—I can't live a life of leisure. But it won't be in the city, and it won't be just for money.'

Russ moved. He took her face in both hands and looked deep into her eyes. 'Is this true, Laurie? Do you really mean it?'

'I really mean it,' she said quietly, and then, at last, he kissed her.

It was a long, lingering kiss that began with gentleness, as if he was half afraid to touch her lips. Laurie felt the softness of his mouth on hers, so different from the kiss she had anticipated, with a strange delight. There was a reverent tenderness that was totally unexpected; yet hardly had she formed this impression than his lips parted and she felt the sensuous flicker of a tongue against her mouth, inviting her lips to open in their turn. Together, their mouths shaped an entrance through which their tongues could pass, seeking, exploring, mingling and touching in tender, intimate caress. And now the softness, the gentleness alternated with a firm, pulsing pressure, a demanding, rhythmic thrust that had her catching her breath and clinging to Russ's shoulders, her fingers tangling wildly in his hair, her body twisting in his arms, her need to be close to him overpowering any other thought.

Slowly, his tongue drew back, softly his lips withdrew from hers. Laurie rested her head against his chest and felt his heart hammering beneath her cheek. Her breath was coming quickly and she felt dizzy, almost faint.

For a long moment they were both silent. Then Russ said huskily, 'You're right, Laurie. We need to talk.'

And now, somehow, it was easy to talk, and she knew she would never be lost for words with him again. With one kiss, he had shown her that she could trust him with her most secret thoughts. With one kiss, she had given herself entirely into his care.

'It was the accident,' she said, her cheek still resting against his heart. 'That day on the lake...when the motor-boat overturned. My mother was skiing behind it, my father was driving. I was watching from the shore, but I never knew what happened. It was all so quick. They were caught up in the propeller, the wire...' She flinched as if she were seeing it again, turning her head into his shoulder, and felt his arms around her, strong and reassuring. 'I never knew what happened,' she repeated in a small, lost voice.

'It was a submerged log,' Russ explained quietly. 'Nobody was to blame, Laurie. It was just a tragic accident.'

Laurie lifted her head and stared at him. 'Is that true?'

'Yes. You can see for yourself in the reports of the inquest.' A frown furrowed his brow. 'Did no one ever tell you?'

'No. My uncle... They wouldn't talk about it. I learned in the end not to ask. But I always had the impression that it was someone's fault—Uncle Tom's, my father's, perhaps one of your family. But I never knew. And I was never allowed to come back.'

'You could have done,' he pointed out, 'when you grew up.'

'I know. But by then such a long time had gone by. It's not easy to go back, Russ, especially when you're afraid of what you might find. And I suppose that's why I never tried to find out what had really happened—never asked for the report of the inquest. I thought I knew—or almost—and I was afraid to know for certain.'

'So it's been haunting you all these years,' he said softly. 'My poor Laurie.'

'I suppose that's why I made such a different sort of life. That and my aunt and uncle's upbringing. They tried to turn me into a different person, Russ, but I was never happy. It was like wearing clothes that don't fit. And when I got engaged to Alec, it was even worse.'

'And then Tom died and left you the cottage.'

'And made me come and live in it. And that's my biggest regret, Russ—that I never really knew my uncle Tom, yet he seems to have known me so well. He must have been hurt that I never came.'

'Maybe. But I think he knew John and Ella Marchant too well to blame you.' Russ moved his hand to turn her face up to his again. 'Laurie...'

'I love you, Russ.' He hadn't said it to her yet, but she knew that for her to make the first declaration was the greatest gift she could give him. And she was no longer afraid of rejection. His kiss had told her everything.

'Laurie, I've always loved you,' he replied, and his voice was so deep that it seemed to come straight from his heart. 'Even when you were a pigtailed brat, following me everywhere, there was something even then that told me you were special. And all through these years—I won't lie to you, there have been women, and I've thought myself in love more than once. But it was never quite right, never all the way. With you—there's no barrier any more.'

'I thought the barriers were too high ever to overcome,' she confessed. 'I thought you despised me.'

'And there were times,' he said, 'when I wanted to. God, how I wanted to!' His eyes were dark as he gazed into hers. 'That day when you came here and I found you wrapped in a blanket on this very rug—Laurie, have you any idea what it did to me to find you here? I wanted to tear the blanket off you and make love to you there and then——'

'You almost did,' she reminded him with a glinting smile.

'I almost did—but I restrained myself just in time. And again, later; I wanted you so badly, Laurie, it was a physical pain. But I knew that, if I gave way to it, just once, I would never be able to leave you. And I thought you were not only engaged to Hadlow,

but also playing some devious game to trap me, to
get your way over the development——'

'It was never *my* way, Russ. I never agreed to that.'

'I know,' he said, and his lips were on hers again.
She felt their warmth, the passion and tenderness that
pulsed in his blood and fired her body. She felt the
hot weakness spread through her limbs, the urgency
of her need to be close to him again, and she moved
against him.

Russ tightened his arms about her, and she felt the
deep murmur of his voice against her skin as he left
her lips to explore her face, her ears, her neck. His
mouth moved down her throat, touched the fluttering
pulse, sought further to find the swelling of her breast.
He touched the throb of her heart, and stroked her
nipple with his tongue, and Laurie shivered and held
his head, her fingers moving convulsively through the
thick, springing hair.

'I know,' he murmured again when they were both
breathless. 'But at that time I couldn't be sure, Laurie.
I didn't want to believe it, but you'd been away for
years; you'd changed. I told myself I was in love with
a dream, a fantasy, someone who no longer existed.
And I dared not take the risk.' His face was tortured.
'Even that last day, when you came to the office and
opened your heart—God, if you only knew how I
ached to touch you that day, to take you in my arms
and kiss the sadness away, love you back into life. But
something stopped me, even then. A feeling that you
still had things to work out, and that you had to do
it alone. There are some things nobody can help with,
Laurie.'

'I know,' she said soberly. 'And you were right. If
I hadn't worked out all those old feelings myself, they

would always have haunted me. But now——' she
looked up at him and her face was bright and open
'—they're not haunting me any longer, Russ. I can
face the truth now. And it's turned out to be so much
less frightening than I thought. Why ever did no one
tell me before?'

He shook his head. 'Who can tell how other people's minds work? Maybe we shouldn't even try,
Laurie. It's their problem. We're going to have enough
trouble just trying to understand ourselves!'

She laughed. 'Not any longer, Russ,' she whispered, snuggling against him. 'There's no risk now.'

He looked down at her, and his mouth twitched.

'No risk? Laurie, you're the biggest threat to my
sanity I've ever known! If I don't have you, I shall
go mad—there's no doubt at all about that. If you
don't stay with me from now on, if you're not mine
for the rest of my life, they'll need to lock me up.
And if you do——'

'If I do? Will you still go mad?' His hand was on
her breast, his lips touching hers, seeking a kiss, but
she drew away to tease him, keeping a whisper of
contact but letting him come no closer. 'Will you,
Russ?'

'Temptress,' he muttered, and her heart leapt as she
heard the passion in his voice. 'Of course I shall—
mad with happiness, with joy. Now—for God's sake,
Laurie, let me kiss you . . .'

He caught her against him with an urgency that she
could no longer resist, nor wanted to. His lips met
hers in a kiss that was a seal on their love, and she
let herself respond, knowing that this was only the
beginning of a lifetime of loving. And, as if Russ recognised too that they had a lifetime before them, he

tempered the urgency of his desire, taking his time as he slowly slid the clothes from her trembling body. Her thick, lined sweater, her ski-pants, her shirt, the silk underwear that kept her warm from wrist to toe . . . all were removed with sensuous care, with caressing fingers, with kisses that swept them both to a height of passion that left them breathless.

Laurie lay before him on the thick rug, the firelight playing on the smooth contours of her slender body, touching her breasts with a rosy light, casting mysterious shadows where his fingers began now to explore. And it wasn't enough for her to be naked; she needed to feel his skin against hers, close and warm, and her need guided her hands to his body, found the buttons and zips, stroked the clothes away from his limbs, as he had caressed her into nakedness. And at last they lay together, limbs entwined, feeling for the first time the rapture of two who belonged together, who fitted as if they had always been intended that way, who were properly and permanently in love.

'You'll never leave me now, Laurie,' Russ murmured with an intensity that lit fresh fires in her heart. His fingers were moving over her, barely brushing her skin, igniting a desire that mounted to an almost frightening passion. 'You're mine now—now and for ever. Mine . . .'

Laurie lay trembling in his arms, dizzy with the force of her feelings. She wanted to lie stretched against him, to feel his skin against hers, to lose herself in the caresses that were waking such rapture. But at the same time she knew that there must be more. And her own hands began to move, touching him with the same gentleness, finding spots that drew a response from him just as his caresses made her whimper and twist against him in an increasing need to be closer, closer. She turned her head, searching for his kiss, moving her body sensuously, wanting to feel the shape of him. She felt him catch her even tighter against his heart. She felt a moment of complete stillness as they lay together entwined, almost afraid to move lest their hunger for each other explode.

And then their two bodies were completely taken over by the emotions and sensations they were waking in each other. Their desire and need in total, mutual accord, they came together in the closest of all embraces, the embrace that lovers had sought since love began. The sky exploded around them in a shower of a million stars. And as Laurie gave herself up to the delight of their love, she knew that this would never, ever end.

Next month's Romances

Each month, you can choose from a world of variety in romance with Mills & Boon. These are the new titles to look out for next month.

THE GOLDEN MASK ROBYN DONALD
THE PERFECT SOLUTION CATHERINE GEORGE
A DATE WITH DESTINY MIRANDA LEE
THE JILTED BRIDEGROOM CAROLE MORTIMER
SPIRIT OF LOVE EMMA GOLDRICK
LEFT IN TRUST KAY THORPE
UNCHAIN MY HEART STEPHANIE HOWARD
RELUCTANT HOSTAGE MARGARET MAYO
TWO-TIMING LOVE KATE PROCTOR
NATURALLY LOVING CATHERINE SPENCER
THE DEVIL YOU KNOW HELEN BROOKS
WHISPERING VINES ELIZABETH DUKE
DENIAL OF LOVE SHIRLEY KEMP
PASSING STRANGERS MARGARET CALLAGHAN
TAME A PROUD HEART JENETH MURREY

STARSIGN
GEMINI GIRL LIZA GOODMAN

Available from Boots, Martins, John Menzies, W.H. Smith, most supermarkets and other paperback stockists.

Also available from Mills & Boon Reader Service, P.O. Box 236, Thornton Road, Croydon, Surrey CR9 3RU.

4 FREE

Romances
and 2 FREE gifts
just for you!

*You can enjoy all the
heartwarming emotion of true love for FREE!
Discover the heartbreak and the happiness, the emotion
and the tenderness of the modern relationships in
Mills & Boon Romances.*

*We'll send you 4 captivating Romances as a special offer
from Mills & Boon Reader Service, along with the chance to
have 6 Romances delivered to your door each month.*

Claim your FREE books and gifts overleaf...

An irresistible offer from Mills & Boon

Here's a personal invitation from Mills & Boon Reader Service, to become a regular reader of Romances. To welcome you, we'd like you to have 4 books, a CUDDLY TEDDY and a special MYSTERY GIFT absolutely FREE.

Then you could look forward each month to receiving 6 brand new Romances, delivered to your door, postage and packing free! Plus our free newsletter featuring author news, competitions, special offers and much more.

This invitation comes with no strings attached. You may cancel or suspend your subscription at any time, and still keep your free books and gifts.

It's so easy. Send no money now. Simply fill in the coupon below and post it to -
Reader Service, FREEPOST, PO Box 236, Croydon, Surrey CR9 9EL.

NO STAMP REQUIRED

Free Books Coupon

Yes! Please rush me my 4 free Romances and 2 free gifts! Please also reserve me a Reader Service subscription. If I decide to subscribe I can look forward to receiving 6 brand new Romances each month for just £9.60, postage and packing free. If I choose not to subscribe I shall write to you within 10 days - I can keep the books and gifts whatever I decide. I may cancel or suspend my subscription at any time. I am over 18 years of age.

Name Mrs/Miss/Ms/Mr _____ EP18R

Address _____

_____

Postcode _____ Signature _____